The Spirit of the School

Ralph Henry Barbour

Alpha Editions

This edition published in 2024

ISBN : 9789361471254

Design and Setting By
Alpha Editions
www.alphaedis.com
Email - info@alphaedis.com

Contents

CHAPTER I
AN OLD ACQUAINTANCE IN A NEW RÔLE

"It's all well enough for you to sit there and grin like a gargle."

"Gargoyle is what you mean, my boy!"

"Well, gargoyle," continued Bert Middleton. "What's the difference? Of course, it's easy enough for you to laugh about it; it isn't your funeral; but I guess if you'd had all your plans made up only to have them knocked higher than a kite at the last minute——"

"I know," said Harry Folsom soothingly. "It's rotten mean luck. I'd have told the doctor that I wouldn't do it."

"But it wasn't his fault, you see. It's dad that's to blame for the whole business. You see, it was this way. The Danas used to live up in Feltonville when I was a kid, and dad and Mr. Dana were second cousins or something, and were sort of partners in a sawmill and one or two things like that. Hansel Dana was about my age, maybe a year younger, and we used to play together sometimes. But his mother used to take him away on visits in the summer, and so we didn't get very chummy. The fact is I never cared much for him. He was sort of namby-pamby, and used to read kid's books most all the time. Mr. Dana died when I was about twelve, and Mrs. Dana and Hansel went out to Ohio to live with relatives. Then this summer dad gets a letter from her saying that she wants to send Hansel to a good school in the East, and asking his advice. And nothing would do for dad but that the little beggar must come here to Beechcroft and room with me! Did you ever hear of such luck? And Larry Royle and I had it all fixed to take that dandy big suite in Weeks. Of course that wouldn't do, for dad says I've got to sort of look after the kid. And as his mother hasn't much money, why, we have to room up here on the top floor of Prince with the grinds and the rest of the queer ones. Look at this hole! Isn't it the limit? One bedroom, about the size of a pill box, dirty wall paper, a rag of a carpet, and a fireplace that I just bet won't do a thing but smoke us out!"

"Oh, I don't know, Bert. I think the place looks mighty swell with all your pictures and truck around. The carpet isn't much, as you say, but then that's all the better; you won't have to be careful about spilling things on it. And maybe What's-his-name will turn out all right."

"A regular farmer, I'll bet! They live in Davis City, Ohio, and I never heard of the place before. He's been going to some sort of a two-cent academy out there, and now he's got it into his head that he can enter the third class here. If he makes the second he'll be doing well."

"You say he plays football?"

"That's what dad says; says he was captain of his team last year. I can just see the team, can't you? And I dare say he'll expect me to get him a place on the eleven here; maybe he expects to be captain again!"

"Oh, well," said Harry, smiling at his friend's woe-begone countenance, "perhaps it won't be as bad as that. And if he's played football at all we ought to be glad to get him. We haven't so much new material in sight this fall that we can afford to be particular. I really think, though, you ought to have gone to the station to meet him, Bert."

"I was busy putting up pictures," answered Bert grumpily. "If he can't find his way from the station up here he'd better go back where he came from."

"I can see where little—say, what the dickens *is* his name, anyway?"

"Hansel."

"Where'd he get it? Well, I can see where he's going to have the time of his young life when he gets here; you're so sweet-tempered, old man!" And Harry Folsom leaned back among the pillows of the window seat and laughed. Bert, sprawling in a dilapidated Morris chair, observed him gloomily.

What he saw was a rather plain-looking lad of seventeen, of medium height and weight, with light hair and gray eyes and an expression of good nature that was seldom absent. Bert had never seen Harry angry; in fact, his good nature was proverbial throughout Beechcroft Academy. He was manager of the football team, and was just the fellow for the office. He possessed a good deal of executive ability, a fair share of common sense, and a faculty for keeping his head and his temper under the greatest provocation.

He differed widely in that respect from his host. Bert Middleton had a temper, and anyone who was with him for any length of time was pretty certain to find it out. Unfortunately, with the temper went a stubbornness that made matters worse.

Except with a few fellows who, in spite of these failings, had stuck to him long enough to discover his better qualities, he was not very popular. His election the preceding year to the captaincy of the football team had come to him as a tribute to his playing ability and not his popularity. He was strikingly good looking, with very black hair and snapping black eyes, and in spite of the fact that he was but eighteen years old, he tipped the gymnasium scales at 170 and stood six feet all but an inch. He was generally acknowledged to have won a place on the All-Preparatory Football Team of the year before, and was without doubt the best full back Beechcroft Academy had ever had. Just at present his expression was not particularly attractive, his forehead being wrinkled into a network of frowns and his mouth drawn down with discontent. Both boys were in their senior year members of what at Beechcroft is called the Fourth Class.

The room in which the two boys were sitting on the afternoon of the day preceding the beginning of the fall term was, in spite of Bert's grumblings, pleasant and homelike. It was well furnished, and if the walls were stained and cracked, the dozens of pictures which Bert had just finished hanging concealed the fact. Through the double window, which formed a recess for the comfortable window seat, the mid-afternoon sun was pouring in, and with it came a fresh breeze and scented from the beech forest which sloped away up the hill behind the school buildings. To the right of the window an open door showed the white unpapered walls of the small bedroom. In the center of the room, beneath an antiquated chandelier, stood a green-topped study table, at the present moment piled high with books awaiting installation in the two low cases which flanked the fireplace. Had you lifted the brown corduroy cushion from the window seat you would have discovered the bench beneath to be engraved quite as completely and almost as intricately as any Egyptian monolith. For Prince Hall is well over eighty years old, and succeeding generations of students have left their marks incised with pocket-knife or hot poker on the woodwork of the rooms.

The residents of Prince Hall professed to be, and probably were, proud of the antiquity and associations of their building. But they couldn't help being sometimes envious of the modern improvements, large, well-lighted rooms, and up-to-date appointments of the rival dormitory, Weeks Hall. Weeks stands at the other side of the academy grounds, with the Academy Hall between it and Prince. The three buildings form a row in front of which the well-kept gravel driveway passes ere it disappears to circle the ivy-covered red brick walls of the laboratory at the rear. Across the drive stand the gymnasium and library, the former a modern brick and sandstone structure more ornate than beautiful, and the latter a granite specimen of the unlovely architecture of fifty years ago, charitably draped in a gown of green ivy leaves, which in a measure hides its rude angles.

Beyond the gymnasium and library the ground slopes in a gentle terrace to a broad meadow, which, known as the Green, is the academy's athletic field, and has two wooden stands in various stages of disrepair. Then comes the winding country road which leads to the village of Bevan Hills a half mile or more away.

Beechcroft is encompassed on three sides by parklike forest, in which the smooth gray boles of beech trees are everywhere visible. As yet their pale-yellow leaves still rustled on the branches, for in the Massachusetts hills the heavy frosts do not come until October at the earliest. To-day, a Wednesday in the last week of September, summer still held sway, and the thick woods were full of golden sunlight and green gloom.

When, having recovered from his mirth, Harry Folsom raised himself and looked out of the open window, he saw spread before him a sunlit vista of yellowing fields, with here and there a white farmhouse amid a green orchard. But the scene was a familiar one, and his gaze passed it by to the village road along which was rattling a barge filled with returning students.

"There's a load of 'em coming around now," announced Harry. "I think I saw Larry out front with the driver."

"That's where he would be naturally," answered Bert, some of the despondency clearing from his face. "For years he's been trying to get Gibbs to let him drive the nags. Some day he will do it, and somebody will get killed. I suppose Hansel was on that load; he wrote he was coming on the 4.12."

"I guess I'll have to stay and see this Fidus Achates of yours, Bert."

"Fidus Achates!" exploded the other. "Fidus poppycock! I wish he was—was———"

"Careful, now!" cautioned Harry with a grin.

"I wish he was at home," ended Bert with a gulp. "I thought I was going to have a good time this year—a decent room with a fellow I liked, not many studies, plenty of time for football and hockey, and—and—now look at me! Stuck up here among the pills with a silly little runt of a country kid for roommate! Oh, a nice cheerful fourth year I shall have!"

"Oh, quit your yowling!" said the other good-naturedly. "You don't know what Dana will be like. For my part I'm ready to like him, if only because you've run him down so. I dare say he will prove to be a very decent sort."

"Oh, decent enough, maybe; but if he's anything like what he used to be, he'll just sit here and read his old books all day and make me nervous. Maybe he'll turn out a grind!"

"But he can't be so awfully fond of staying indoors and reading if he was captain of his football team."

"Shucks! I'll bet I know what sort of football he plays! His team probably averaged a hundred and twenty pounds and played back of the village livery stable. I'm going to have the dustpan ready to sweep up the hayseed when he takes his hat off!"

"Well, he will be here in a minute," laughed Harry, "and then we'll know the worst. If he's as bad as you picture him, I don't blame you for being——"

He was interrupted by a knock at the door. The two exchanged questioning glances, and then Bert called "Come in!" The door swung open and a tall, well-built youth entered, set down a suit case, and looked inquiringly from Harry to Bert.

"I'm looking for Bert Middleton," he announced, "and I guess you're the chap, aren't you?" He looked smilingly at Bert, who had arisen from his chair and was observing the newcomer with a puzzled frown.

"'I am looking for Bert Middleton,' he announced."

"Why, yes; but—you—look here, you're not Hansel Dana, are you?"

"Yes"—the two shook hands—"I suppose I've changed some since you saw me last. So have you, for that matter. You're heaps bigger, but that black hair of yours looks just the same."

"Yes, you have changed," answered Bert. "I'm glad to see you." He turned to where Harry was smiling broadly at his amazement. "This is Mr. Folsom, Hansel; Mr. Dana. We—we were just speaking of you when you knocked."

"Yes," said Harry, shaking hands heartily, "Bert was telling me how glad he was you and he were to be together." He shot a malicious glance at Bert and was rewarded with a scowl. The newcomer looked shrewdly at Bert's innocent countenance and smiled a little.

"Rather a pleasant room we've got, Bert," he observed.

"Oh, fair for a cheap one."

"Is this a cheap one?" asked the other, opening his eyes. "I thought the rent was sixty dollars."

"So it is. Over in Weeks some of the suites are two hundred."

"Hum; things come high here, don't they? Is this your furniture?"

"Yes, most of it; one or two things are rented."

"I didn't bring much. I didn't quite know what was wanted. But I suppose I can get things here, can't I? I'd like to do my share."

"You can't get much here," answered Harry. "You'll have to go to Boston, I guess. But I don't see that you two need much else."

"We need another easy chair," said Bert, "and a rug or two wouldn't look bad. If we've got to live in a garret like this we might as well be as comfortable as we can."

The newcomer's eyes narrowed a trifle.

"All right," he answered quietly. "I'll see what I can do." He went to the window and stood there a moment looking out over the sunlit landscape and peeling off a pair of very proper tan gloves. Harry and Bert exchanged glances. Presently he turned and, tossing his gloves aside, sat down on the window seat, took one knee into his hands, and looked about the room with frank interest.

Hansel Dana was seventeen years old, a tall, clean-cut boy with very little superfluous flesh beneath his neat, well-fitting gray suit. Despite his height he looked and was heavy. His hair was brown and so were his eyes, and the latter had a way of looking straight at you when he talked that was a little bit disconcerting at first. Harry Folsom, who, being quite out of the running himself, had a deep liking for good looks, mentally dubbed Dana the handsomest fellow in school. His nose was straight, his mouth firm without being thin, and his chin was square and aggressive. There was a liberal dash of healthy color in each cheek. As for his attire, there was little to confirm Bert's prophecies. He wore a white negligee shirt, a suit of gray flannel, low tan shoes, and when he had entered had worn a gray cloth cap. The clothes were not expensive, but, as Harry ruefully acknowledged to himself, looked better than did his own garments, for which he had paid possibly three times as much. Altogether Hansel Dana made a very presentable appearance. And his manner, a pleasing mixture of self-possessed ease and modesty, was not the least of his charm.

"He looks to me," mused Harry, "like a chap who knows his own mind and won't be afraid to let somebody else know it. And if he can play football the way he took his gloves off and set that bag down, I fancy there'll be something doing. Also, unless I'm much mistaken, 22 Prince Hall has got a new boss!" And he smiled to himself at the idea of Bert Middleton knuckling under to anybody.

Hansel had plenty of questions to ask, and he asked them. And the others supplied the answers, Bert becoming quite genial under his new roommate's implied deference to his experience and knowledge. Harry, who fancied he could see a rude awakening ahead for Bert, enjoyed himself hugely. Presently the talk worked around to football, as it inevitably will where two or more boys are gathered together when frost is in the air, and Bert inquired whether Hansel played.

"Yes, I've played some," was the answer. "We had a team out home at the academy. They made me captain last year. We had pretty good fun."

"Did you win your big game?" asked Harry.

"No," Hansel answered carelessly. "We lost that; lost plenty of others, too, for that matter. But we were pretty light, had no coach, and had to pay our own traveling expenses besides; that made it difficult, for lots of the fellows couldn't afford to pay fares, and so when we went away from home it was mighty hard work to get a full eleven to go along."

Bert glanced across at Harry with a "I-told-you-so" expression.

"Yes, that must have made it hard," laughed Harry. "Well, you must come out for the team to-morrow. By the way, where did you play?"

"Last year at left end; before that at right half."

"That's bad," said Bert. "We're pretty well fixed in the back field and we've got slathers of candidates for the end positions. What we need are men for the line. But I guess you'd be too light there. What's your weight?"

"A hundred and fifty-eight when I'm in shape."

"Well, maybe you'd have chance at tackle," said Bert dubiously.

"Don't believe I could make good there," answered Hansel. "I guess it's end or nothing in my case. By the way, when do we get supper?"

"Six," answered Harry.

"I'm starved. Didn't get any lunch in Boston because my train from the West was over an hour late. Well, I guess I can hold out another hour."

"You're going into the third class, Bert says," said Harry.

"Yes, if I can pass the exams, and I guess I can. Latin's the only thing I'm afraid of."

"Well, get Bert to bring you over to my room to-night. You take the exams to-morrow, you know, and maybe we can give you a few pointers. Bring him over, Bert, will you? I'll see you in dining hall, maybe. I want to run across and see whether Larry has turned up. Did you notice a big fellow on the front seat coming up from the station?"

"Yes, weighed about a thousand pounds. Who is he?" asked Hansel.

"Larry Royle. He's in your class. He lives in the big house across the road. His dad owns pretty near everything around here. Larry's our center, and he's a crackajack, too. I'll run over a minute. By the way, Bert, shall I find that dustpan for you?"

And Harry disappeared beyond the door, laughing.

"He seems a nice sort," said Hansel warmly.

"He is; he's a mighty good chap. He's manager of the football team, by the way, and if you want any favors you'd better stand in with him. You know, I dare say, that I'm captain this year?"

"Yes, I think your father said something about it in one of his letters."

"Yes; well, of course, I'll do what I can for you if you want to make the team, but—there's a bunch of pretty swift players here, and so—if you shouldn't make it, you know, you mustn't be disappointed. Of course, I can't show any favoritism; you understand that; and——"

"Oh, that's all right!" interrupted Hansel with a smile. "Don't you bother about me; I'll look out for myself, Bert. If I thought there was any likelihood of you showing favoritism I wouldn't go out. But I don't believe there's any danger—at least, not unless you've changed a whole lot. Perhaps you don't recall the fact, Bert, but you used to make life pretty uncomfortable for me when we were kids back there in Feltonville. I suppose you didn't mean anything particularly, but I haven't quite forgotten it."

"Pshaw!" said Bert uncomfortably. "You were such a little sissy——"

"And I don't suppose," the other continued calmly, "that you were overpleased to have me for a roommate. For that matter, neither was I. But there wasn't any help for it, and so I thought we'd make the best of it. What can't be cured, you know, must be endured. I dare say we'll get on pretty well together. At least, we know where we stand. You'll find me pretty decent as long as you behave yourself. But"—Hansel arose and went toward the bedroom—"but none of those old tricks of yours, Bert."

He disappeared, and Bert, sitting fairly open-mouthed and speechless with amazement, heard him pouring water into the bowl.

CHAPTER II
HANSEL DECLARES FOR REFORM

Two days later Hansel Dana had officially become a student at Beechcroft Academy, one of a colony of some one hundred and forty-odd youths of from twelve to twenty years of age, about half of whom lived in the two school dormitories and half in the village or in the occasional white-painted and green-shuttered residences along the way to it. (In Beechcroft parlance the former were called "Schoolers" and the latter "Towners," and there was always more or less rivalry between them.) Hansel had passed his entrance examinations with a condition in Latin which he must work off during the fall term, and he was very well satisfied. Harry told him, in the words of Grover Cleveland, that "it was a condition and not a theory which confronted him," but Hansel didn't have any doubt as to his ability to work it off before the Christmas recess.

He had also meanwhile passed another examination, and that without conditions. The candidates for the school eleven, by which term the first team was known, had assembled on the afternoon of the first day of school, and never before, according to Mr. Ames, had there been so many of them; and never, he had also added to himself, had they been nearly so unpromising. Out of a possible one hundred and forty-odd students, seventy-one, or practically one-half, had reported for practice on the green. Of the number five had played on the last year's team, while many others had been on either the scrub or the class elevens. Hansel, because of an examination in mathematics, had not been able to reach the green until the first practice was almost half over. He had reported to Bert Middleton, and had been ungraciously sent to one of the awkward squads composed of the candidates from the entering class. But he hadn't stayed there very long. Mr. Ames, making the round of the squads, had watched him for a moment and had thereupon sent him into the second group, which was under the instruction of a big, good-natured boy whom Hansel recognized as the Laurence Royle of whom Harry Folsom had spoken. The first day's practice consisted principally of exercises designed to limber up stiff muscles, and proved most uninteresting and disappointing to many of the new candidates. After doing a quarter of a mile jog around the cinder track, the fellows were sent up to the gymnasium, where their names and weights were taken down by the manager. On the second afternoon the unpromising candidates were weeded out, and definite teams—first, second, third, and fourth—were formed; and Hansel found himself one of sixteen lucky fellows constituting the first.

The coach was Mr. Ames, instructor in French and German. He had played football and baseball during his college days at Harvard, and had, in fact, been an all-round athlete. He was a young man, very popular with the students and very successful in handling them, either on the gridiron or in the classroom. During his five years as coach Beechcroft had won three football games from Fairview School, her dearest enemy, and had lost two; had been defeated three times in baseball, had tied one game and won one; had been generally successful on the track, and in the two years that hockey had been played had been twice defeated. The physical training was looked after by Mr. Foote, the director of the gymnasium. Undoubtedly Beechcroft could have done better in athletics had she had a professional trainer and additional coaches, but there was little revenue from athletics and almost no support from graduates, and as a consequence what money was obtained for athletic expenditure came from the students themselves and was insufficient for anything more than the items of equipment, field maintenance, and traveling expenses. Under the circumstances, it was felt that Beechcroft did very well.

Mr. Ames believed that in Hansel the football team had a find of no small importance. The boy evidently knew football from the ground up, had weight, speed, and brains, and promised to develop into one of the best men on the team. He confided his belief to Bert and Harry one afternoon after practice was over, and even Bert was forced, seemingly against his will, to agree with him. Harry was enthusiastic, possibly because he had discerned Hansel's abilities at their first meeting, and so felt a sort of proprietary interest in him.

"He's got end cinched," declared the manager. "Cutter and Grant will have to toss up to see which one of them goes to the scrub. I knew the first moment I set eyes on the fellow that he could play the game."

"Well, if he's a find he's the only one that I know about," said Bert. "There isn't anyone else in sight who threatens to become famous."

"That's so," agreed Mr. Ames. "The new men are a poor lot from the football standpoint. But there's some good track material in sight."

"Hang your old track material," laughed Bert. "What I'm looking for is a few good heavy linemen."

After the coach had taken himself off, Bert and Harry went up to the latter's room in Weeks.

"How are you and Achates getting on together?" asked Harry when he had pushed Bert into an easy chair and thrown himself among the window cushions.

"Oh, all right, I guess. I told you he had a grudge against me, didn't I, because he says I used to haze him when he was a youngster?"

"Yes, but of course you didn't really do such a thing," laughed Harry.

"You dry up! I dare say I did tease him a bit; he was such a milksop, you see. But I think it's mighty small of him to remember it all this time!"

"Yes, I suppose so, but—oh, I don't know; he seems sort of funny in some ways, don't you think?"

"Yes, he's woozy, the silly dub! And I know all the time that he's sort of laughing at me up his sleeve because I told him not to be disappointed if he didn't make the team."

"Did you tell him that?" laughed Harry.

"Yes; I didn't want him to think he could get on just because he roomed with the captain; you know lots of fellows would have thought that."

"Ye-es, but I don't think Dana's that kind."

"Maybe not; I know he isn't, in fact. But I didn't then. Gee but he *can* play!"

"You'd better believe it, Bert! I'll bet he'll turn out the best end in years. Why, the chap can run like a gale of wind, and as for putting his man out—" Words failed him. "Well, I'm glad you two are chummy; it makes it better, eh?"

"We're not exactly chummy," answered Bert with a frown, "but we get on all right. He attends to his affairs and I attend to mine; we don't have much to say to each other—yet."

"Pshaw, don't be nasty, Bert. He'll be decent if you will, I bet. You know you have a temper sometimes, and——"

"I don't remember things a thousand years, do I?" asked the other angrily. "Temper! Who wouldn't have a temper when——"

"There, there, old chap! Don't get waxy with me. If you do I'll throw you out of the window!"

Whereupon a scuffle ensued, and Bert's ill temper passed.

Bert's description of the existing relations between the occupants of 22 Prince was a true one. He and Hansel "got on all right," but there wasn't much chumming. Football seemed to be the only topic which could induce conversation. Sometimes an hour passed in the evening during which not a word was exchanged across the study table. Bert would have been glad to let bygones be bygones, for he liked Hansel, if only because of the latter's ability to play football; Bert would have found a warm corner in his heart for the sorriest specimen of humanity imaginable had the latter been able to play the game well. But he wasn't one to make advances even had there been encouragement, which there wasn't. Hansel was always polite, always amiable, but, so far as Bert could see, didn't care a row of pins whether his roommate came or went. Life at home wasn't enlivening to Bert in those days, for he was very dependent upon the society of others for happiness; solitude had small attraction for him and silence still less. As a result he spent most of his time, when study was not absolutely necessary, away from his room.

On the second evening following the conversation recorded with Harry, however, he was at home; study to-night was incumbent. He sat at one side of the table and Hansel at the other. For the better part of an hour each had been immersed in his books and not a word had been said. Finally, Bert pushed his work away, stretched, yawned, and looked at the little clock on the mantel. As the clock was never known to be right, the resulting increase in knowledge wasn't valuable. He knew plaguy well it wasn't twenty-six minutes to seven! Hansel raised his head and glanced across at him.

"Going to knock off?" he asked politely.

"Yes, I guess so." He pined for conversation and wished heartily that the other would stop studying and talk. "What you worrying over?"

"Latin," was the laconic reply, as Hansel's head bent over the book again.

"Find it hard?"

"Yes, I hate the foolish stuff."

"Well, I never found it hard; but math has me floored."

"That so?"

"Yes."

Silence, during which the untruthful clock ticked loudly.

"How are you with math?"

"Fair, I guess; mathematics don't bother me much."

"Wish I could say that. Did you ever hear the yarn they tell on Billy Cameron?"

"No, I don't think so," was the polite and uninterested response. But Bert wasn't to be silenced.

"Well, you know Billy's about twenty or twenty-one. He went to Bursley for about a hundred years before he came here. They got tired of trying to teach him anything and so he left there and showed up here. At least—well, that's one reason. The other reason is that we needed a good half back, and Billy was open to inducements."

Hansel's eyes came away from his book and he began to show signs of interest.

"What sort of inducements?" he asked.

"Oh, the usual, you know; tuition paid by popular subscription and a nice comfortable place as waiter in dining hall, where he doesn't have to do much and gets his meals free."

"Oh," said Hansel thoughtfully.

"It isn't supposed to be known, of course, but I guess it is. I guess folks don't make the mistake of thinking Billy is here to improve his mind. He's a good chap, but his mind will never trouble him—that way! And of course the only reason they let him stay at Bursley so long was just because he was one of the best players on any school team and they needed his assistance. Well, as I was saying, the story goes that some one said to Billy one day— and, by the way, he's been in the second class ever since he came here, and that's a year this fall—some one said to him: 'Say, Billy, how are you getting on with your studies?' 'Oh,' said Billy, 'pretty fair.' 'That's good. Find it easy going, do you?' 'Well, I don't know about that,' says Billy. 'The field's pretty rough in places.'"

"Hm," said Hansel. He didn't even smile, and Bert regarded him disgustedly. Bert thought that a pretty funny yarn.

"Look here," demanded the other after a moment of silence, "do you mean to tell me that that fellow is here just to play football and that the school is paying his expenses?"

"That's about it," answered Bert in surprise. "Why?"

"I don't like it," said Hansel decisively.

"Don't like it? Well—well, what can you do? Why don't you like it?" Bert was genuinely astonished.

"I don't like to think that that sort of thing is done at the school I go to," answered the other firmly. "When I found I was coming here to Beechcroft I was proud of it. I had heard of the school all my life and had always wanted to come here, but never expected to be able to. Beechcroft has stood for me for everything that's fine and high and—and noble in school life, and now you tell me that it's no better than any of the little mean sneaky schools out West that give free tuition and board to any chap who can kick a football or run around the bases! That's why I don't like it, Bert."

"Well, don't you let the fellows hear you calling Beechcroft mean and sneaky," said Bert indignantly. "If you do you'll get laid out."

"Isn't it?" asked Hansel quietly.

"No, it isn't!" exploded Bert. "You needn't judge Beechcroft by your little two-by-twice schools out West. What if Cameron does get helped along by the fellows? If we're willing to do it it's our affair. He's a *bona fide* student at the academy, and no one can say he isn't."

"But I say it," Hansel replied calmly.

Bert glared at him across the table as though on the point of inflicting blows. But Hansel's steady untroubled gaze deterred him, and he contented himself with flinging himself out of his chair and seeking the support of the mantel.

"Then you lie!" he retorted hotly.

"I don't think I do," was the answer. "You're not looking at the thing fairly and squarely, Bert. Here's a fellow who hasn't come here to prepare himself for college, who isn't paying his own tuition, and who wouldn't be here a day if he wasn't a swell football player. And you call him a '*bona fide* student'!"

"Of course I do! He's taking a regular course at the school and keeping up with his studies——"

"How?"

"What?"

"I asked how?"

"Same as you and I, I suppose."

"But you've said yourself that he couldn't stay at Bursley, and anyone knows that Beechcroft is three times as hard as Bursley. Who's coaching him?"

"What's that got to do with it? Aren't lots of the fellows coached?"

"Maybe; but who is coaching Cameron?"

"I don't know; it's none of my business. And it's none of yours either, Hansel."

"Yes, it is. Cameron has no business here; at least, he has no business playing on the school football team, and you know it."

"Oh, don't be a silly ass!" said Bert angrily. "You're too blamed particular. Why, great Scott! lots of the schools have fellows on their football and baseball teams that aren't any better than Cameron. Look at Bursley!"

"Maybe lots of them do, but that isn't any reason that we should. Besides, I don't believe many of them are like that. Bursley may be, but how about Fairview?"

"She'd take Cameron in a minute if she could get him!"

"I don't believe it, Bert."

"You don't have to. Maybe you know a lot more about it than I do!"

"Well, anyway, I think it's a pretty poor piece of business. It isn't as though we couldn't get a winning team out of a hundred and fifty fellows, either; that makes it worse; we're dishonest when there isn't the least excuse for it. You needn't tell me we couldn't win from Fairview one year out of two without this Cameron fellow. Are there any more like him here?"

"You find out! I've told you all I'm going to. You make me tired, putting on airs as though Beechcroft wasn't as good as any old school out where you come from."

"She's better than some of them," answered Hansel calmly, "but I don't know of a school out my way with half the reputation that Beechcroft has that would do such a thing."

"Rot!"

"It's so, just the same."

"Well, let me tell you one thing; if you go around talking the way you have to-night you'll get yourself mighty well disliked—and serve you right! You needn't think we're going to take a lot of nonsense like that from a fellow who comes from a little old village academy that no one ever heard of!"

"What does Ames think of it?" asked Hansel irrelevantly.

"You'd better ask him."

"I will. And I'll tell you what else I'm going to do," continued Hansel, with a look in his steady brown eyes that Bert found disquieting. "I'm going to do away with that sort of thing at Beechcroft, if not this year, then next. Will you help me?"

"Me?" gasped Bert, thoroughly taken aback. "No, I won't!"

"Well, I didn't suppose you would, although as captain of the team you ought to be the first one to do so. I'll just have to go ahead without you."

Hansel drew his book toward him and seemed to consider the subject closed. Bert regarded him a moment in silence. Somehow he felt worsted, impotent, and in the wrong. And the feeling didn't improve his temper.

"A fat lot you can do," he growled wrathfully.

"You wait and see," was the placid response.

CHAPTER III
MR. AMES TELLS A STORY

The next day was Sunday. For a week the weather had been suggestive of early December rather than the first week in October, but to-day it had relented and there was a warmth and balminess in the air that would have coaxed a hermit out of his cell. There was nothing of the hermit about Hansel and so he required very little coaxing. There was church in the morning at Bevan Hills, and the boys who lived on the grounds—the "Schoolers," as they were called—walked thither in two squads under the care of Mr. Ames and Mr. Foote. They were required to walk, if not exactly in procession, at least in an orderly manner on the way to church, but coming home, as there was a full hour between the close of service and the time for dinner, restrictions were largely removed, and the fellows loitered or made excursions afield about as they chose. Mr. Ames's squad was always the larger of the two, since he was rather more popular than Mr. Foote, and allowed the boys greater liberty, at the same time maintaining, seemingly with little trouble, a far better discipline. As Harry Folsom explained to Hansel on the way back:

"You don't mind doing what Bobby tells you to, somehow. But Foote—oh, I don't know; you always feel like worrying him; and he's not a half bad sort, either. Bobby, though, seems more like one of us fellows; I guess he understands what a fellow wants and—and all that, you know."

The sun was pretty warm on the way back, and when they left the road to take the well-worn path across the green—a route which cut off a full quarter of a mile of the distance between village and school—some one proposed a halt for rest before they tackled the slope.

"That's a good suggestion," answered Mr. Ames, seating himself on the grass in the shade and fanning himself with his hat. "I wanted to make it myself, fellows, but I was afraid you'd think I was getting old and infirm."

The fellows followed his example and threw themselves down on the grass out of the sunlight, all save one or two who roamed away into the little patch of forest across the dusty road to see how the chestnut crop was coming along. For a time the conversation, what little there was, was half-hearted and desultory. The explorers returned with an encouraging report, and proceeded to cool off. Presently, one of the older boys sat up and turned to the instructor.

"Tell us a story, Mr. Ames," he said, and there was an immediate and unanimous indorsement of the request. Mr. Ames smiled and looked at his watch.

"I guess you fellows have heard all of my yarns," he answered.

"No, sir, I haven't!"

"Nor I, sir!"

"I'd like to hear them all over," added a third.

"Well, I won't inflict that calamity on you," laughed the instructor. "But let me see. What sort of a story do you want?"

"A funny one, sir."

"Tell us about the time you went to New Haven as sub and got in in the last half and won the game."

"Come now, Strafford, I never did that! You've let your imagination run away with you. I'll not tell you anything more except fairy stories if you twist things around that way."

"Mr. Ames," answered the boy earnestly, "you did win that game, sir. I heard a man at home telling all about it last summer. He said Harvard was going all to pieces when you went in at quarter and that you just shook the men right together and just *made* them score that time. He said if it hadn't been for you the game would have ended nothing to nothing."

"Oh, I guess he was just having fun with you," said Mr. Ames somewhat embarrassedly. "I don't remember anything like that."

"He wasn't telling me about it at all," protested the boy. "I was just there and heard it. I wanted to tell him that you were our coach here, but I didn't know him."

"It was just as well, then, under the circumstances," laughed the instructor. "What was the chap's name; do you know?"

"Yes, sir, it was Higgins; a big, tall——"

"Mortimer Higgins! Is that so? I haven't heard of him for a long time. We called him 'Mort' at college. And, by the way, if you still want a story I can tell you one, and it's about this same Mort Higgins. It isn't exactly a funny story, but it's a true one; and if you don't believe it, why, Strafford here will show you the hero!"

"That's fine!"

"Go ahead, sir!"

"Shut up, you fellows! Mr. Ames is going to tell a story!"

"Well, I'll try and make it short," began the instructor, "for it's getting along toward dinner time. Let's see, now. Mort was in the class ahead of me, and I never knew him until my sophomore year. He was a junior then. I wonder if I can describe him to you, so that you'll see him as I did. He was tall—a good six feet, I guess—and a bit lanky and ungainly. He came from one of the Carolinas—North, I think, and was sort of slow and careless in his movements, used to throw his shoulders all around when he walked, and when he shook hands with you, you felt as though your fingers were tied to a pump handle and the pump was going until it ran down. He had black hair, coarse and long and all rumpled up. It used to fall down over his forehead, and he had a way of brushing it aside with his big hand as though he was trying to dash his brains out. He had a long nose and a long neck, and he always wore those turndown collars that made his neck look longer than it really was. His eyes were gray, I think, and were always laughing at each other; at least, that's what I used to think. His mouth was big and sort of—what shall I say?—sort of loose, and altogether he was about as homely a chap as there was in college. But his homeliness was of the kind that attracted you. When you first saw him you said to yourself: 'My, isn't he homely! Talk about your mud fences—' Then you looked again and began to think: 'Well, now, he may be homely, but bless me if it isn't becoming to him!'

"He had a queer sort of a drawl that made his most serious remarks sound funny; Mort only had to open his mouth to start you smiling. He was awfully good-hearted and good-natured; he'd do anything for you if he didn't absolutely dislike you; and I don't believe Mort Higgins ever really disliked anyone. He was one of the sort that can always find good in folks. No matter how mean a chap was, Mort could always point out a few good things about him. And, on the other hand, I don't suppose there was a fellow in college who didn't like Mort—whether they knew him or not. But most everybody did know him. Mort never waited for introductions. If he ran up against a fellow and had anything to say he said it; and no one ever resented it; you couldn't with Mort Higgins. You only had to glance at him to see that he was simply bubbling over with human kindness.

"He was a smart scholar; did all kinds of things in his last year, and graduated with honors. But that isn't what I started out to tell about. There used to be lots of stories around Cambridge in those days about Mort. Some of them were true, I guess, and a good many of them weren't. One of them was about Mort and his school club."

"Tell it, sir, please," said Harry Folsom.

"Well, at Harvard we had a good many clubs and societies, you know. If you were from the South, you joined the Southern Club; if from California, you joined the California Club. If you went to school at Exeter, you belonged to the Exeter Club; and so on. Every school, pretty near, was represented by a club, which met once a month or once a fortnight, as the case might be. I think Mort belonged to the Southern Club, but that wasn't enough for him. His friends all had their school societies, and so Mort thought he ought to have his. It seems that he was prepared for college—or so he said; I have my doubts—at Turkey Creek Academy. I suppose it was some little village school in the backwoods of Mort's native State. Wherever it was, it soon began to become celebrated. One day there was a notice in the *Crimson*—that's the college daily, you know—saying that it was proposed to start a social club of Harvard men who had attended Turkey Creek Academy, and that a meeting for that purpose would be held that evening in Parlor A of one of the hotels in town. Well, for a couple of days everybody was talking and joking about Turkey Creek Academy; it got to be a byword. A week later there was another notice in the *Crimson* announcing a meeting of the Turkey Creek Club in Mort's room. Then came the announcement the next day—of course it was a paid advertisement—that at a meeting of the Turkey Creek Club Mortimer Higgins had been elected president, Mort Higgins secretary, and M. Higgins treasurer. And then Mort appeared, wearing a green, yellow, and purple hatband on his old gray felt hat, and a pin about as big as a half dollar on the front of his vest. He said they were the insignia of the Turkey Creek Club. He had a grip, too, and he'd show it to you by shaking hands with himself. For, of course, Mort was the only member.

"Well, he had lots of fun, and so did everyone else. 'Turkey Creek' spread through college until you heard it everywhere. The principal drug store got up a 'Turkey Creek College Ice,' and a quick-lunch place advertised a 'Turkey Creek Egg Sandwich.' Mort got the name of 'Turkey' for a while, but it didn't stick, probably because 'Mort' was shorter. He kept up the Turkey Creek game all the rest of the year. Every now and then there'd be a notice in the *Crimson*; and everyone used to watch for them. Finally, though, it dawned on the *Crimson* that it was being used to perpetrate a joke, and it turned Mort down; the *Crimson*, you know, is the most serious paper in the world outside of the *Congressional Record*. After that he used to post his notices up on the notice board in the union and the gym. One day there was a notice saying that at half-past twelve the Turkey Creek Club would have its photograph taken on the steps of Matthews Hall. Of course everyone who could get there was on hand, and sure enough there was the photographer waiting. And pretty soon Mort steps up, dressed in his best clothes and wearing his green and yellow and purple hatband and his club pin, and stands on the top step and folds his arms.

You can imagine the howl that went up as Mort faced the camera as serious as a judge!"

"I thought you said it wasn't a funny story!" gurgled one of the audience when the laughter had died down.

"That's so, but that wasn't the story I started out to tell," answered Mr. Ames. "I was going to tell about Mort's baseball experience, but I guess I've wasted too much time and we'll have to let that go until another day."

"Oh, go ahead, sir! It isn't late!" The instructor looked at his watch.

"Well, maybe there's time if I hurry up with it. When Mort came to Harvard he'd never seen a game of baseball played, and he fell in love with it right away and went out to try for his freshman team. He didn't make it, but he wasn't discouraged, and the next year he made the sophomore team; they let him play at right field, I think. The next year he went out for the varsity nine. He slipped up on that, but he made the second. And somehow he began to get a reputation as a heavy hitter, and, as the varsity was weak at batting, they nabbed Mort and took him to the varsity training table. But he spent most of that spring on the bench, for while at times he'd just about knock the cover off the ball, he wasn't a bit certain, and there was no telling whether he'd make a home run or strike out; and usually it was a case of strike out with Mort. And in the field—they tried him at left and then at right, and it didn't seem to make any difference to Mort—he was a good deal of a failure. If he ever got his mitten on the ball he clung to it, but he didn't seem to be able to judge the direction of flies, and like as not would be four or five yards out of the way when the ball came down. But he tried terribly hard, and everyone liked him, and so he stayed with the team, even though he didn't get into any of the big games.

"In his senior year he was out again, and the coach, who was a new man, got it into his head that Mort could be taught to field. And he was taught, after a fashion. At least, he did a whole lot better that spring and only disgraced himself a couple of times. But those times were enough to queer him, and back to the bench he went. Now and then, when the varsity was up against a weak team, they'd let Mort take a hand, and it was a pretty sure thing that he'd stir up some excitement by getting a couple of two-baggers or a home run before he was through with the enemy's pitcher. We used to laugh and cheer like anything when Mort went to bat. But the real fun came when he got to base. At base running he was like an elephant in a forty-yards sprint. To see him try to steal was more fun than a circus. He'd get the signal and start off at a lope for second. The batsman would strike at the ball without hitting it, the catcher would throw down to second, and second baseman would stand there with the ball in his hand and wait for

Mort to come galloping up to be tagged out. Oh, it was beautiful! And Mort would come ambling back to the bench smiling and unruffled.

"Well, that's the way things stood when the team went to New Haven for the second Yale game. We'd won the first at Cambridge, and if we could get this one we had the series. I was playing short. It was a pitchers' battle all through. We managed to get two runs in the second inning, and after that there was nothing doing until the sixth, when Yale's first man was hit with the ball and stole second on a bad throw down. The second man went out on a pop fly, and the third struck out. The next man got his base on balls, and then there was a three-bagger that brought in two runs. So the score stood two to two until the last of the eighth. Then came a bunch of errors—I had a hand in it myself—and finally a squeeze that brought in another run. We settled down then and our pitcher struck out the next two men, and we went to bat in the first of the ninth with the score three to two against us.

"I was first up and managed to get a scratch hit, beating the ball to first by about an inch. I had my instructions to wait for a sacrifice and I waited. But the next man was struck out. Then came a long fly into the left-fielder's hands, but I managed to sneak down to second on the throw-in. There were two out and it looked as though there was going to be a third game to the series that year. The Yale stands were cheering incessantly and beating drums and having a high old time. The next man up was our first baseman. He was the slugging kind of a batter; if he hit the ball he made good, but he was easily fooled. Well, this time he wasn't fooled. He cracked out a clean base hit over second and I started home. But there was a fine, swift throw to the plate and I had to go back to third—and I didn't get there any too soon! And meanwhile the other fellow had got to second. And there we were; a man on third and a man on second, two runs needed to win, and the weakest batter on the team up! That was our pitcher. He was a bully pitcher, but, like nine pitchers out of ten, he couldn't bat a little bit. I was feeling pretty sore when I saw him pick up his bat and start for the plate. But he didn't get there, for the coach called him back, and suddenly there was a burst of cheering from the Harvard section. They were sending Mort Higgins in to bat for him.

"Well, that was all right, thought I, for Mort couldn't do any worse than the man whose place he had taken. But I didn't look for any luck, for the Yale pitcher was one of the best on the college diamond that year, and we had made only four hits off him in the whole game. I wondered whether I could make a sneak for the plate and tie the score. Mort struck at the first ball and missed it. He looked surprised, and the Yale crowd howled. Then he let the next one go by and the umpire called it a strike. My heart went down into my boots. Then Mort refused the next one. I can still remember the feeling of relief with which I heard the umpire say 'Ball'! The Yale pitcher tied himself up again and unwound and the ball shot away. And then there was a nice, clean-sounding *crack*, and I was racing for the plate. The ball went whizzing by my head along the base line, but I didn't stop to see whether it was going to be fair or foul. And neither did the man behind me. We put out for the plate like sixty, and we both made it ahead of the ball, which had struck about a foot inside the line. There were things doing in the Harvard section about that time, I tell you, fellows!"

"And did Mort get in, too?" asked some one eagerly. Mr. Ames laughed.

"No," he answered, "Mort didn't score. Catcher threw the ball back to second, and second ran half way over to first and met Mort coming along like a human windmill, waving his arms and pawing the earth."

"And Harvard won?"

"Yes, four to three. We shut Yale out in her half of the inning. And that's how Mort Higgins saved the day. Come on, fellows; we'll have to hurry or we'll be late for dinner."

"Gee!" said one of the boys, as they scrambled to their feet and started up the path, "that was bully! I'd like to have been there, Mr. Ames!"

"Well, I was rather glad to be there myself," answered the instructor with a reminiscent smile.

After dinner Hansel met Bert and Harry in front of Weeks, and the latter called to him to join them in a walk. Bert didn't look as though he was especially pleased with Harry's procedure; since their discussion of ethics the evening before, he had treated Hansel rather coldly. But Hansel went along, and presently Bert forgot his resentment and the three spent a very pleasant two hours along the bank of the lake. Naturally, the talk soon got around to the subject of football, and the team's chances of success in the final contest of the year—that with Fairview—were discussed exhaustively. As though by tacit consent, both Bert and Hansel avoided a reopening of the controversy regarding Billy Cameron. On the way back to school, Harry Folsom let fall an allusion to the "raid," and Hansel asked for information.

"Oh, you'll know all about it in a day or two," laughed the football manager. "It's due to happen either to-morrow or Tuesday night. You want to get into your old clothes and be prepared for trouble in bunches."

"But what is it?" insisted Hansel.

"It's when the Towners come up here after supper and try to get on to the steps of Academy Building and cheer. I don't know when the thing started, but it's been the custom for years. They try to take us Schoolers by surprise and rush the steps before we can stop them. Our play is to keep them away, or, if they get there, to put them off. But if they once make the steps they're pretty sure to stay there. It's a lovely rough-house, isn't it, Bert? Last year they did about as they liked with us, and all we could do was to bother them. They stood there on the steps and cheered for themselves for about half an hour. When they started home, though, we got at them in fine style and chased them all the way back to the town."

"I got a peach of a crack on the side of the head last year," said Bert, with a trace of pride in his voice.

"Well, some of the Towners got a heap worse," laughed Harry. "Simpson had most of his clothes torn off him before he got home. Simpson was their leader," he explained for Hansel's enlightenment.

"And Poor! Do you remember?" cried Bert. "He lived at Mrs. Hyde's, and two of us fellows chased him inside the yard and he tried to dive through an open window and the window came down on him when he was half way through and pinned him there. We didn't do a thing to him!"

"But how do you know when the raid's going to occur?" asked Hansel.

"We don't," Harry replied. "We only know that it usually comes the first of this week. We have to be on guard. But we've got a dandy scheme fixed up for this time. I'd tell you, Dana, but it's a sort of a secret; we don't want it to get out, you know."

"That's all right," said Hansel. "I suppose I'll learn about it in time."

"I wouldn't be surprised," said Bert, "if you learned about it to-morrow evening. I have an idea that they mean to raid then, for Royle told me yesterday that young Gates, one of the Towners, told him that it was going to come off Tuesday. That looks to me as though they wanted to put us off the track."

"Sure! That's just what it means," Harry answered with conviction. "Anyhow, we'll be ready for them whenever they come. They won't find us asleep the way they did last year, you can bet on that!"

And, as it proved, they didn't.

CHAPTER IV
SCHOOL AGAINST TOWN

"I don't believe they're coming to-night, after all," said Bert disappointedly, as he turned away from the window. He was dressed in his oldest trousers and wore a canvas football jacket. Hansel, propped on one elbow on the window seat, was similarly attired. It was long after supper, and twilight was fast deepening to dark. The stretch of road visible from the study window which they had been watching for almost an hour past was already merging itself with the surrounding gloom.

"We couldn't see them now," muttered Hansel, "if a whole army of Towners marched along it."

"I'm going to light up," said Bert disgustedly.

"Go ahead," his roommate answered. "I guess you're right, Bert. It's to-morrow night, after all. I wish, though, that they'd come and have it over with. I can't study now after having the raid in mind all day."

"I don't feel much like it myself," Bert replied as he scratched a match loudly, "but I guess I'll have to do it if I don't want to get into trouble. That's the worst about being on the team. Other fellows can get behind a bit in their studies and no one thinks anything about it, but just let one of the football——"

"*Hist!*" called Hansel sharply. "Blow out that match and come here, Bert!"

The match arched through the darkness like a miniature comet and fell in the grate with a shower of tiny sparks, while Bert, blinded by the sudden transition from light to gloom, went stumbling and bumping to the window.

"What is it?" he asked hoarsely.

"I don't know," answered Hansel doubtfully. "Perhaps I was mistaken."

"Well, well, what was it?" the other demanded impatiently, as he peered out into the darkness.

"See that light stretch over there between the grand stand and the woods? Well, I could have sworn that I saw three figures cross there coming this way."

"You couldn't have," said Bert. "It's too dark to see anything. You imagined it, probably. Besides, what would three fellows be doing alone? There are eighty-four Towners this year, and when they come they'll come in a big old bunch. I tell you what, Hansel; what you saw was probably some of our pickets. Gordon and Stark and two or three others are down that way somewhere."

"Maybe that was it, then," said Hansel. "Only I was sure I saw something. And they seemed to be sort of crouching along as though they didn't want to be seen."

"It was probably some of the pickets coming in. It's eight o'clock; they won't be up to-night."

"Well, let's go out for a few minutes," said Hansel. "I can't study now. I don't see what good we could do up here, anyhow, if they did come!"

"Well, we wanted them to think we weren't expecting them. That's why we told the fellows to stay in their rooms and keep the gas lighted until they heard the alarm given. If they came sneaking up here and found us all standing around the yard waiting for them they might take it into their head to go back again. But it's so dark now I guess they couldn't see us, so come on. I'll light up first, though. What the dickens did I do with that box of matches, I wonder? I had it a minute ago. See if I left it on the window sill there, will you? Here—oh, hang it! I've spilled them all over the floor!"

He scratched one of the troublesome matches under the edge of the mantel and turned toward the gas fixture. With one hand on the key of the nearest bracket and the other holding the flaring match he stood motionless, staring at Hansel's face uncertainly visible in the half light.

"What was that?" he cried softly.

"What? I didn't hear——"

"Listen!"

"School this way! School this way! School this way!"

Bert threw the match into the grate and leaped toward the door.

"Come on!" he cried. "They're here!"

As he dashed out of the door, Hansel close behind him, the corridor and stairway were noisy with the tramping of many feet.

"Raid! Raid!" was the cry echoing through the building. Doors were crashing shut upstairs and down, and the valiant defenders were taking the stairs three or four at a time. Bert and Hansel joined the hurrying throng, and in a trice found themselves outside in the darkness. Overhead a few stars twinkled wanly. The unlighted bulk of Academy Building rose before them at a little distance and toward it they sped. But the cries of *"School! School! School this way!"* came from farther along toward Weeks. The steps of Academy were empty, and after a moment's indecision, Bert and Hansel and a few others who had followed them turned away and hurried toward the rallying place. A crowd of some half hundred fellows had already gathered in front of Weeks, and in the dim light from the open doorway Hansel made out Harry Folsom, who seemed to be in charge of affairs.

"That you, Bert?" he cried, as they ran up. "They're down there on the road. They'll be in sight in a minute. They've got Johnny Parrish and they almost got Jones, but he escaped and gave the alarm. He says there doesn't seem to be more than fifty of them. I say let's meet them at the gate, break them up, and chase them back. What do you say?"

"All right! Come on!"

With a cheer the party moved toward the gate, a hundred yards away. Hansel, between a couple of fellows he didn't know, for he had lost track of Bert in the confusion, felt his heart pounding excitedly. As they reached the edge of the school grounds, a cheer started from the head of the little army, and those behind, taking it up, pressed forward. At a little distance, a black blur in the surrounding gloom, were the invaders. Finding themselves discovered, they set up a defiant cheer of *"Town! Town! Town!"*

Then they moved forward again.

The defenders halted just outside the gates and awaited them silently. Nearer and nearer came the Towners until, when a dozen yards away, they broke into a run and, cheering wildly, dashed into the ranks of the Schoolers. In the instant confusion reigned. Cries of "School!" and "Town!" rang out. Hansel, in the center of the school army, was swayed hither and thither, jammed in between laughing, shouting fellows. For a moment the defenders gave before the impetus of the rush, but for a moment only. The Schoolers recovered and moved forward, the foe giving before them. Suddenly Hansel found himself toward the front of the school group, and a big town boy had him by his sweater and was striving to push him aside, shouting his battle cry of "Town! Town!" deafeningly in his ear. Hansel panted and shoved; those behind came to his rescue, and his opponent went struggling back again.

Then Hansel was in the thick of it. Hither and thither swayed the struggling mass, shouting, laughing, panting; now and then a sweater or jacket would give with a ripping sound, or a cap, the property of some misguided youth, went sailing away into the darkness. It was impossible to distinguish friend from foe, and so Hansel set his teeth and shoved and pushed forward with the rest of his side. There were no blows struck, or if there were, they were harmless and unintentional. Hansel was surprised at the good humor which prevailed in spite of the excitement. The Towners were yielding foot by foot now, and the cheers of the defenders arose triumphantly into the night air. But just when it seemed that in another instant the foe must break and run, a new and disturbing sound reached the defenders. From behind them, in the direction of Academy Building, came the loud challenging cry of "Town! Town! Town!"

"By Jove!" cried Harry Folsom. "They've fooled us! Back to the steps, fellows!"

The school forces turned in dismay and raced through the gate and back along the curving drive, the invaders, cheering lustily, close upon them. Hansel, as he ran, recollected the forms he had seen crossing behind the athletic field. The Towners had tricked them! While their main force had attacked openly by the road a smaller force had crept around by the woods on the other side and were now, judging from the sounds, in possession of the coveted steps! Yes, there they were, some twenty-five or thirty of them, shoulder to shoulder, on the steps of Academy, cheering loudly.

"Town! Town!" they shouted in unison.

"School! School! Drive them off!" cried the defenders as they raced toward them.

But at their heels came the main army of the invaders, cheering and laughing, and the Schoolers were literally caught between two fires. Up the first steps dashed the Schoolers and sought to pull down the enemy in possession of the stronghold. In a moment chaos reigned!

Up and down the steps flowed and ebbed the tide of battle. Towners were dislodged, but others sprang through the ranks of the school and took their places. Hansel fought his way to the front only to be hurled unceremoniously over the edge of the steps onto the turf. He picked himself up and sprang again into the swaying, shouting mass. It would have been much simpler had it been possible to distinguish friends from foes. As it was, the Towners when challenged shouted "School!" in order to reach their comrades on the steps, and the Schoolers, following suit, cried "Town! Town!" in order to fool the enemy.

Confusion reigned supreme then when the doors of Academy Building suddenly crashed open behind the little group of Towners holding the top steps, and the disconcerting yell of "*School! School! School!*" broke forth behind them. It was the Towners' turn to be surprised. Out from the doorway dashed a handful of defenders and, shoving and shouting mightily, they took the invaders in the rear and scattered them like chaff. With cheers of triumph the Schoolers below took the place of the invaders, and in a moment the tide of battle had turned effectually. Quickly the Schoolers gathered their scattered forces on the steps and about them, while the Towners rallied again at the corner of the gymnasium.

There was a moment or two while hostilities ceased, and in that time Harry and the other leaders laid their plans hurriedly. Then, with a cheer, half of the defenders hurled themselves upon the invading forces. For a while the result of the charge was doubtful, but at last the enemy's ranks were pierced and divided. Part of them fled along the road in front of the gymnasium and part scattered across the terrace, making for the green and the path to the village. Had they remained together they might easily have retired in good order and gained the village without further loss of prestige. But the sudden attack from the rear had dismayed them, and now, disorganized thoroughly, their only thought was to reach the village in safety. It was every man for himself, and the fleeing Towners were soon strung out without form or discipline, the fastest runners heading the rout.

Hansel was among the body of pursuers which charged across the terrace and the green in the wake of that portion of the invading force which had luckily chosen the shortest way home. Until the road was reached the Towners held well enough together to be able to resist any real attack. But once on the road the flight became a mad scramble for safety, in which every fellow thought only of himself. Then the pursuit caught up with the laggards and either sent them into the woods or fields or captured them and subjected them to such indignities as smearing their faces with handfuls of dust or depriving them by force of jackets or sweaters. As every fellow was careful to wear only the oldest things he possessed, the loss of the garments was more embarrassing than serious. Before the edge of town was reached, the pursuit had slackened. Some two dozen Schoolers, Hansel among them, paused, panting and laughing, and listened to the cries dying away on the road ahead of them. It was much too dark to distinguish faces, but Hansel recognized one or two fellows by their voices, and soon discovered that Harry Folsom was there.

"My," said some one, "I haven't any breath left! Let's go home, fellows."

"Get out!" said another. "What we want to do is to wait here for the rest of the Towners, and when they come jump out on them and scare them into fits."

"That's so! They'll be along in a minute if they stick to the road."

"Oh, they'll stay on the road all right. Listen! They're coming now!"

"Get down, fellows," called Harry softly, "so they won't see us!"

There was a minute of silent suspense while the group crouched in the darkness at the side of the road. Then came the *pat, pat* of footsteps up the road.

"It's only one," Harry whispered. "Wait till a bunch of them comes along."

The runner jogged past, dimly visible, panting wearily, and silence followed. Then more footsteps sounded in the silence and in a moment a half-dozen fellows, very tired and short of breath, trotted up, and——

"Now!" whispered Harry.

With blood-curdling screams the party in ambush leaped out upon its quarry. The latter sought to escape but were quickly surrounded and captured; all save one, a big fellow named Cartwright, who managed to beat off the enemy and put a dozen yards between them and himself before they started in pursuit. Then Hansel and two other Schoolers went after him. Weary as he was, it was a short chase, and they soon had him at bay against the fence at one side of the road. But he didn't propose to submit meekly to capture.

"You fellows touch me and you'll get hurt!" he panted angrily. "Keep away now."

"It's Billy Cartwright!" exclaimed one of Hansel's companions. "You're our game, old chap, so you might as well give in."

"You let me alone," was the reply, "or there'll be trouble!"

"He wants to fight," said the Schooler. "You ought to be ashamed of yourself, Billy, to lose your temper. Look at us; we're not angry!"

"That's all right, but if you fellows think you can rough-house me, you're mightily mistaken. I'm going home."

"Oh, no, you're not, Billy. We're not through with you yet!"

"Keep off, I tell you!"

"Come on, fellows!"

The three sprang onto him together, and for a while there was a very lively tussle there by the fence. Cartwright fought like a tiger, thoroughly angry. Hansel received a blow from some one's elbow that dazed him for a moment, but he clung hard to the victim's legs, and in a moment Cartwright was down and they were on top of him listening to a torrent of abuse and threats.

"Oh, shut up," said Hansel, a little out of temper now himself, since his nose was still aching with the blow he had received. "Can't you take a joke? What's the matter with you, anyhow?"

"Did you get him, fellows?" called Harry from up the road.

"Sure," replied one of Hansel's companions, "but he put up a dickens of a fight. What'll we do with him?"

"Wanted to fight, did he?" asked Harry as he came up with two or three other fellows. "Who is it? Cartwright? Oh, Billy never could take a joke. We ought to show him how. There's a brook over here somewhere. Do you think we can find it?"

"Easy!" answered some one. "Where is he? Hello, Billy! Still feeling scrappy?"

Cartwright replied that he was, only he didn't confine himself to a simple statement of the fact. The Schoolers listened to him disgustedly.

"You make me tired, Billy," said Harry at last. "Shut up or we'll half drown you! Say, fellows, let those dubs go and come over here. There's something doing."

A moment later Cartwright was lifted over the fence, no easy task for his captors, since he still struggled fiercely, and was half pushed and half carried across the meadow. No one knew just where the brook lay, and it was finally discovered by one of the Schoolers stumbling into it.

"Are you sure this is it?" laughed Harry.

"Sure!" replied the fellow succinctly as he wrung the water out of his trousers. "And it's good and wet, too!"

"All right then, fellows. Lift him up and when I give the word drop him gently into the seething caldron. All ready? Then—let—him—go!"

He went. There was a splash, a torrent of choking remarks from Cartwright, which was drowned by the laughter of the Schoolers, and then he was crawling out on the other side, dripping and somewhat subdued.

"Good night!" called Harry mockingly.

There was no reply save a growl as Cartwright stumbled away across the meadow toward town.

"Next time, Billy," called another of his friends, "I advise you to keep your temper."

Still laughing, the group made its way back to the road and turned toward school. As they went, now and then a group of two or three

Towners passed. But they had had their troubles already and the fellows allowed them to go unmolested. But they were forced to listen to many jeering remarks, such as:

"'Rah for the Towners!"

"Great cheering on the steps, fellows!"

"Come again! Always glad to see you! And bring your friends; you'll need them!"

Ordinarily, the fellows were required to be in the dormitories at nine o'clock and to have their lights out at ten, but on Raid Night the rules were relaxed, and so when they reached the campus, their cheers were answered by a throng in front of Academy, and a jubilation meeting was held there. Every few minutes late comers straggled up with new tales to tell. Almost everyone had some trophy of the chase in the shape of captured garments. The crowd was in a fair way to cheer itself hoarse when Mr. Foote appeared on the scene.

"Fellows, you must stop this now," he said. "It's almost eleven o'clock."

They jeered good-naturedly and then sent up a cheer for him, and presently dispersed to the dormitories, Hansel, and possibly many others, to dream of the evening's exciting adventures.

CHAPTER V
HANSEL MEETS PHINEAS DORR

For a week life progressed quickly and busily for Hansel. His mornings were fully occupied in the class rooms, and at three o'clock each afternoon he was on the green dressed in football togs ready for the practice. He was at right end now, having displaced King of last year's second, and there was little doubt in the minds of the other players and Mr. Ames that he would be able to hold the position against all comers. His playing was a revelation to many of the candidates. There was not a faster, harder runner on the team, and none could equal him at tackling. And with these physical abilities went a mental alertness, coolness, and judgment that enhanced and perfected them. Mr. Ames struck right end from the list of positions to be filled and turned his attention to other points in the line.

Back of Hansel played Cotton at quarter, Curtis at left half, Cameron at right half (the Three C's they were called), and Bert Middleton at full back. At center was big Royle. But the rest of the positions, excepting right end, were still filled only tentatively, and every day the linemen were shifted or dropped out to make room for promising candidates from the second squad.

Naturally, Hansel soon made the speaking acquaintance of Billy Cameron; and he found himself at a loss to understand that youth. Hansel made the mistake of imagining that a fellow occupying such an equivocal position in the school must necessarily exhibit signs of depravity or meanness. And a more harmless, better-natured youth than Cameron it would have been hard to find. He was popularly believed to be twenty years of age, and looked it. He was rather heavy of build, but wonderfully quick on his feet, and was an ideal plunging half back. He had tow-colored hair and twinkling blue eyes and was rather handsome. He was good-natured to a fault, had good manners, which seemed to have been acquired rather than inherited, and had never been known to indulge in dirty playing. And Hansel never heard a foul word pass his lips. The former, after a week's acquaintance with Cameron, discovered that he would have to revise his preconceived ideas of that youth. He even found himself entertaining a mild liking for him, and, since his notions of right and wrong were pretty sharply defined, it worried him not a little. And he began to wonder what was to become of Cameron if he succeeded, as he had determined to, in setting school sentiment against that youth.

During that week Hansel realized that, in spite of his expressed confidence in his ability to bring about reform, he had a difficult task ahead of him. He had not spoken as yet to Mr. Ames on the subject—he was purposely putting that off until later—but the one or two fellows to whom he had mentioned the matter, had disappointed him. Folsom, for instance, of whom Hansel had expected sympathy at least, if not actual assistance, had only laughed good-naturedly.

"It isn't quite right, of course," said Harry, "but then it's done all over the shop. Even the faculties wink at it, and in some schools they lend a hand. If you're going to change things, Dana, you'll have to begin at the bottom."

"Where's that?" asked Hansel.

"At the top," answered Harry with a laugh. "I mean the colleges. You see, we school fellows take our cues from the colleges. And when they hire athletes we think we can do the same thing."

"But do they—here in the East? I thought——"

"Yes, they do; that is, lots of 'em do. It's usually done on the sly, but we knew of it. Why, thunderation! don't they come here every year to get our best men and offer 'em all sorts of easy snaps if they'll go with 'em to—well, any of the colleges, pretty near! What's Perkins doing at —— this year? Steward of an eating club with a salary that's big enough to pay all his expenses and let him run an automobile! And Perkins's dad is a carpenter over in Whitby; never saw a fifty-dollar bill in his life, I'll bet! It isn't right, as you say, Dana, but—what can you do?"

"I don't know yet," answered Hansel, "but I can do something. And if you won't help——"

"Oh, I haven't said that," replied Harry easily. "You find your method, you know, and maybe I'll take a hand. Only," with a meaning laugh, "don't get too near home, Dana."

"How do you mean?"

"Well, I'm manager of the team this year and I want to win. So don't meddle with any of my men; see?"

"Yes," answered Hansel thoughtfully, "I see. Only—I may have to."

Harry laughed good-naturedly and clapped him on the shoulder.

"I'll risk it, I guess. You mean well, Dana, and I—well, I hope you succeed—next year. Come around and see me."

Anderson, captain of the baseball team, to whom Hansel sought and obtained an introduction, told him he was wasting his time, and refused to lend even moral assistance. Field, president of the fourth class, looked bored, and said it was a good work and he hoped Hansel would succeed, but—er—it was a difficult undertaking; "Every fellow doesn't look at the matter in the same light, you know, and—er—well, come around again and let me know how you get along."

To add to the difficulties, Hansel was practically an outsider. While he was a member of the third class, yet he knew scarcely six men in it. The other members had been together for two years and had formed their groups and coteries long since, and to gain admittance to these was likely to prove no easy task. Had Hansel come up to Beechcroft from some nearby school it would have been different; he would scarcely have failed to find others who had attended the same institution and who would have taken him up and, possibly, secured him admission into their clubs. But no one at Beechcroft had ever so much as heard of the little academy out in Ohio from which Hansel had migrated, and so there were no outstretched hands to welcome him into the inner circles of class life. At the end of his second week at Beechcroft Hansel was well acquainted with Bert and Harry, knew most of the members of the first squad well enough to talk to, and had a nodding acquaintance with some or six other chaps. Of course he had no intention of allowing such a state of affairs to continue for long, and he had a shrewd idea that after the first one or two games, by which time he would have become identified as one of the school eleven, he would find it fairly easy to make acquaintances. But meanwhile he felt rather outside of things and, had he had time, would probably have experienced qualms of homesickness. He wrote more letters to Davis City, Ohio, during that fortnight than during any subsequent period of like length, and his mother's replies, full of the trivial but vastly interesting happenings of the little town, were happy events. The first offer of assistance, in what Harry jocularly called his "crusade against vice," came finally from an unexpected quarter.

Harry's invitations to visit him were frequent, but so far Hansel had not entered the study in Weeks Hall since the evening of his arrival. And so, on the afternoon preceding the first football game, when the practice was light and over early, he accepted the invitation. He had not yet abandoned hope of winning Harry over to active membership in the "crusade"; and, besides, he liked the football manager better than any of his few acquaintances. Harry roomed alone in a suite of study and bedroom on the second floor of Prince. The study was plainly but richly furnished and was a revelation to Hansel. The walls were covered with dark-green cartridge paper, against which hung a scant half-dozen good pictures. Over each door was a shelf holding a cast. The floor was painted and bare save for a few rugs in quiet tones of olive and gray and dull red. A handsome mahogany study table took up the center of the apartment and a few easy chairs with good lines stood about. These, with a comfortable divan, heaped with pillows, practically comprised the furnishings of a room which was at once simple and in good taste. Harry was at work at the table when Hansel entered.

"Busy?" asked the latter. "I just came in to chin a bit, and so if——"

"Busy? Not at all; merely studying," was the reply. "It isn't often any fellow has the decency to come in and interrupt me when I'm studying. First thing I know I'll have brain fever! Sit down and rest your face and hands." He pushed his books and paper aside, laid down his pen, and leaned back in his chair. "How's the crusade coming on?"

"I'm afraid it's at a standstill at present," answered Hansel with a smile. "The fact is, I'm still recruiting."

"Like Falstaff," suggested Harry. "How many have you got?"

"Only you so far."

"Me? No, you don't! I refuse to be drafted. I—I've water on the brain and can't fight. Scratch me off, if you please, general."

"All right, but I'll get you yet," said Hansel cheerfully. Harry looked across at him thoughtfully. Then:

"Hanged if I don't believe you will, confound you!" he answered. Then he laughed. "Why don't you give it up until next year, Dana?" he asked.

"So as not to interfere with Cameron?"

"No, honestly I wasn't thinking of him. But look here, old fellow, to speak plainly now, if you go ahead with it, the first thing you know they'll set you down as a crank and—and that isn't pleasant in a school like this. Give a fellow a name for—for peculiarity here and it's all up with him."

"All up with him how?"

"Well, in a social sense, I mean. The fellows fight shy of you and you get left out of things, societies and offices, you know. I don't want to seem cheeky, Dana, but really there's a good deal in what I say. And—and you're the sort of a chap that can have a pretty good time here and do a whole lot if—if you don't get—peculiar."

"I dare say you're right, Folsom——"

"Cut it out; no one ever calls me that."

"All right, then I won't either. I've been thinking myself that very likely the fellows would put me down for several kinds of a crank, but—really, I don't know why I should feel so—so strongly about this thing; but I do; and there you are. And I guess if I am in for getting a reputation for peculiarity, as you call it, why, I'm in for it, that's all. Anyhow, I haven't any idea of backing down."

"No, I didn't suppose you had," said Harry with conviction. "I only thought it was my duty in a way to—er—mention the matter to you."

"I'm much obliged. And, to prove it, there's a captaincy awaiting you whenever you are ready to join."

"Confound you," laughed Harry, "you're a regular—what-you-call-it—proselytist!"

"It's an awful sounding word," said Hansel, "and I don't quite know what——"

There was a knock on the door, and, at Harry's command to enter, there appeared a youth at whom Hansel gazed with interest. He was apparently of about Hansel's age, but slighter, with a thin, pinched nose, a straight, serious, and determined mouth, too large for symmetry, rather long and very dark-brown hair, which needed trimming, and a pale face from which a pair of keen, attractive hazel eyes smiled across at Harry. He was far from handsome, but there was, nevertheless, that about him, an expression of kindliness and honesty, an atmosphere of purposeful courage and manliness that had made him one of the best-liked fellows in school. His clothes were neat but the worse for wear. The straw hat which he held had evidently seen more than one summer, his shoes were patched from heel to toe, and the very low collar, encompassed by a wispy black silk tie, threadworn and long since out of date, emphasized the length and thinness of his neck. Hansel's first conclusion was that the fellow needed a square meal, the next that he needed several.

"Hello, Phin!" cried Harry heartily. "I'm mighty glad to see you. Where have you kept yourself since school began? By the way, you fellows haven't met, have you? Phin, this is Mr. Dana; Mr. Dorr—Mr. Dana. Dana's in your class, Phin; just entered. I want you to do what you can to get him into the crowd; will you?"

"I shall be very pleased to," said Phineas Dorr, as he shook hands with Hansel, "though I don't suppose there's much I can do." He had a rather deep voice which scarcely seemed to belong to such a thin body, but there was a quality to it which attracted Hansel just as it did everyone else. The three sat down, and Harry repeated his question.

"Where have you kept yourself? Why haven't you been around?"

"Well, I've been rather busy, Harry. I'm boarding at a new place this year, and there was a good deal to do about the house."

"I see. Where are you?"

"At Mrs. Freer's, near the Congregational church."

"Freer's? I thought I knew them all, but——"

"She's a newcomer; just moved in a couple of weeks ago. The fact is, she's from Lowell, where I live, you know; she's a friend of ours, sort of a—a relative, you know."

"Oh, and you've been helping her fix up, eh? Putting down her carpets for her, running errands, and everything else, I suppose. You're too blamed good-natured, Phin."

"Well, she's a relative and so, of course, I've had to help, Harry. She's—she's very kind."

"Like all of 'em, I guess; gives you a hole under the eaves and soaks you three dollars for it!"

"No, I've got a very comfortable room this year; much better than the one I had at Morton's."

"Well, I should hope so! That was the limit!"

"I didn't pay much."

"You shouldn't have paid anything," said Harry grimly. "Mrs. Morton ought to have paid you. Well, I'm glad you came around; glad to see you back again. You know you said last year you weren't certain of getting back."

"I know; there was some doubt about it, but I managed it—so far. That reminds me of what I came to see you about."

"You're a mean dub, Phin," said Harry sadly. "I thought you came because you wanted to see me again."

"So I did, as you know," said the other with one of the infrequent smiles which made his thin face almost good-looking. "But there was business, too, in it. You see, Harry, I'm under rather more expense this year, and I'm trying to find a little work to help out. I've got a few furnaces in the village, but I need more."

"My dear chap, I don't own a furnace," laughed Harry kindly. "You can search me!"

"I know," answered Phin, echoing Hansel's laugh. "What I want is to do any odd jobs you may have."

"Odd jobs? For the love of Mike! what sort of odd jobs, you crazy duffer?"

"Well, carpentering and things like that. You know I'm pretty handy with tools. If you want any shelves put up or things like that, I can do them a good deal cheaper than the town carpenter will."

"Oh!" Harry looked thoughtfully about the apartment. "Well, I don't see anything right now, Phin, but if I ever want any tinkering you may be sure I'll send for you."

"Thanks." Phin looked across at Hansel. "And I'd be glad if you would let me do anything of the sort for you, Mr. Dana," he added.

"Surely," said Hansel. "Glad to have you."

"Hold on, man! You're not going?" asked Harry.

"I must," replied Phin, who had arisen and was moving toward the door. "I'm soliciting trade, you see, and I've got a good many fellows to look up yet. I'll come around some other day and see you, Harry. Very glad to have met you, Mr. Dana. I shall be around to see you in a day or so, if I may? Thank you. I know several fellows I think you would like to meet and who will be very glad to meet you. By the way, Harry, there's another thing." He paused with his hand on the doorknob. "You don't happen to know of any fellow who is looking for a nice room without board in the village, do you?"

Harry shook his head.

"If you do, just mention Mrs. Freer's to him, will you? She's got a very comfortable downstairs room which she will rent very cheap. Good-by; see you both again."

And Mr. Phineas Dorr passed out.

Hansel looked across at Harry inquiringly.

"Poor old Phin," muttered Harry, smiling and shaking his head.

"Why?" asked Hansel. "What's the matter with him?"

"Nothing, except that he's as poor as a church mouse. I don't believe he's seen a beefsteak near to in his life. He looked bad enough last year, but this year he's thinner than ever."

"Who is he? Tell me about him."

"Well, he's Phin Dorr, Phineas Dorr, though no one ever calls him that. He comes from Lowell, and is working his way through; looks after furnaces, cuts grass, mends everything he can find to mend, and, in winter, shovels snow. He's a wonder as a Jack-of-all-trades, is Phin. He entered last year. He's in your class. He managed to get a scholarship last year, and I guess he'll get another this year; if he don't, I fancy he'll be up against it pretty hard. Every fellow knows Phin—and likes him; in fact, I wouldn't be surprised if he had more influence than any chap here. He's one of the best fellows ever made."

"Has he folks?"

"A mother only; poor as poor, they say. His father had money once, I heard, and lost it. He's dead now. I shall have to fake up something for him to do for me, though goodness knows I don't need any shelves."

"I do," said Hansel. "I want a big, long one."

Harry observed him smilingly.

"Well, don't let him suspect you are doing it for charity, old man; Phin won't stand for that. Besides, I thought—" He paused in some embarrassment.

"Thought I was poor, too, you mean? So I am, but he's a heap sight poorer. And—and I like him."

"Every fellow does. Phin, in spite of his old patched clothes, is one of the best things we have here. And, by the way, Hansel, you tell Phin about the crusade. He's sort of peculiar himself."

"I will," said Hansel.

CHAPTER VI
THE CAUSE GAINS A CONVERT

The next afternoon Beechcroft played Kensington High School. Kensington's men were light, and Bert's warriors had no difficulty in piling up seventeen points in the first fifteen-minute half. Only old-fashioned formations were used, and there was little in the game to awaken the onlookers to enthusiasm. In the second half the team was materially changed, Bert, Conly, and Cotton giving their positions in the back field to substitutes, and Hansel and two other linemen retiring. They hurried through the showers and rubdowns in the gymnasium and were back on the side lines in time to watch most of the second half.

The leavening of subs in the Beechcroft team made a good deal of difference. The line developed holes and the back field was slower. Several times Kensington made her distance, and Bert, who was entertaining hopes of reaching the Fairview game with an uncrossed goal line, displayed signs of uneasiness. The substitute who had taken Cotton's place at quarter did not prove as good as expected, and twice a poor pass resulted in a fumbled ball. On each occasion luck stood by the home team and the pigskin was recovered, but there was no knowing what might happen the next time.

Kensington was unable to make gain consistently through the line, and so, having obtained the ball on a punt, she set to work trying the ends. The first attempt, a run outside left end, was nipped in the bud by King, who got through and nailed the high school captain behind his line. But the next try worked better. There was a long pass from quarter to left half and the interference, admirably arranged, swung wide and rushed across the field. Cutler, who had taken Hansel's place, was put out of the way without difficulty, and when the Beechcroft right end penetrated the interference and brought down the runner, the latter had managed to reel off a good fifteen yards and the ball was in the middle of the field. The little group of high school supporters yelled delightedly. The next play was a straight plunge at center, which came to nothing. This was followed by a cross-buck at left tackle and a yard had been gained. The Kensington quarter fell back for a kick on the third down, but the ball went to right half and again there was a gain, this time around King's end. For the first time during the game, Kensington was inside Beechcroft's forty-yard line.

Kensington's spirits rose. She hammered at left tackle for a yard, secured two more between right guard and tackle, and made her distance through left tackle. On the side line, Bert scowled wrathfully and Harry made notes at Mr. Ames's directions in a memorandum book. It began to look like a score for Kensington. But her next three attempts only netted four yards, and Bert sighed with relief as the substitute quarter dropped back for a kick. Royle passed well, but Kensington, massing her attack at the right of the line, broke through, and when the ball left quarter's toe it struck full on the breast of a leaping high school player, bounded back, and went rolling toward Beechcroft's goal line. Like a streak of lightning, the Kensington captain was on it, rolled over, and found his feet again and raced toward Beechcroft's goal. There was but a scant thirty yards to go, and for a moment it seemed that he had every chance of making it. Two Beechcroft pursuers were shouldered away by the hastily formed interference, and another white line passed under the feet of the speeding high school captain. Then a light-blue jersey broke from the straggling pursuit, left the others as though they were standing still, and bore down like a flash on the runner with the ball. It was Cameron. He eluded the first of the interference, was shouldered aside by the second, recovered instantly, and gained at every stride on the Kensington player. They were both inside the ten-yard line now and Cameron's arms were stretched forth for the tackle. But surely he was too late! No, for just short of the line he dived forward, his arms locked themselves about the opponent's knees, and they crashed to earth together a yard from the last white streak!

Bert smiled contentedly. Hansel, nearby, shouted his delight. It had been a heart-stirring run, and Cameron's tackle was one of the cleanest and hardest seen on the green that fall. Beechcroft lined up on her goal line and Kensington hammered despairingly at her, only to lose the ball on downs and race back up the field under a punt which this time was got off without hindrance. A moment after the whistle sounded and Beechcroft's goal line was still uncrossed. As he trotted up the terrace toward his room, Hansel reflected ruefully that the fellow against whom he had undertaken to arouse school sentiment was the one who had saved them from being scored on. His task looked more difficult every day; while, to make matters worse, each day brought him an increase of liking and admiration for Cameron.

"Hang it all!" he muttered. "I wish he wasn't such a decent chap!"

The next day was Sunday, and in the afternoon he set forth for the village to find Phineas Dorr. It wasn't an easy task, for no one seemed to know where Mrs. Freer lived. Finally, he remembered that Phin had said something about the Congregational church, and after that it was easy. The house was a tiny white cottage with green blinds and a general look of disrepair. The paint was so thin that in many places the warped clapboards showed through it. But in spite of its neglected exterior, which, after all, was somewhat mitigated by the cleanliness and neatness of the little front yard, the interior proved very homelike and attractive. Hansel didn't penetrate farther than the hallway on that occasion, for Phin was not in, but what he saw from there pleased him. Everything was scrupulously fresh and neat. The strip of rag carpet in the hall looked as though it had just come in from the line after a hard beating, and the dainty dimity curtains in the parlor made him think, somehow, of his own home, although he couldn't recollect any similar window draperies there.

The person who answered his ring was a sweet-faced little woman of perhaps forty-five years. She wore spectacles, and the near-sighted way in which she peered up at Hansel seemed to add to the homely kindliness of her expression. Even had Phin not mentioned the fact that Mrs. Freer was a relative of his, Hansel would have guessed it from the resemblance between the two. Mrs. Freer was very sorry Phineas was out, and begged Hansel to leave his name and a message, if there was one. So Hansel scribbled a note on a slip of paper and asked her to give it to Phin.

"I would like to have you come and put up a shelf for me when you have time," he wrote. "If you can call to-morrow afternoon between half-past two and three I shall be at home. Yours, Dana, 22 Prince."

That evening he mentioned to Bert his intention of having a shelf put up above the couch in the study. He expected opposition, and was not disappointed.

"A shelf?" exclaimed Bert. "What do you want a shelf for?"

"My books."

"But you've only got about a dozen! What do you want a six-foot shelf for, I'd like to know?"

"I may get some more."

"Well, it'll make the place look like the dickens!"

"Oh, no, it won't. I'll get Dorr to enamel it white."

"Hang it, Hansel, I think this place looks bum enough as it is without any homemade truck stuck around!"

"Oh, you'll like it when it's up," answered the other cheerfully.

"I'll bet I don't! Besides, if you've got money to spend on furnishing the room, you'd better buy a chair with it."

"We've got chairs enough. Besides—Dorr needs the money."

"Oh!" said Bert, with a sudden change of expression. "So that's it, eh? Why didn't you say so? If you're doing it to help Phin——"

"I'm not; at least, not altogether."

"Bet you are," said the other more amiably. "He was up here last week with a yarn about wanting to do carpentering. I guess he has a pretty tough time of it." There was a moment's silence. Then, "Look here," he said, "I'm going to pay half, you know."

"No, I'll pay for it. It's my affair."

"How is it? This study's as much mine as it is yours, isn't it?"

"Of course."

"Well, then I pay half on improvements."

"But I thought you didn't think that shelf was an improvement," said Hansel slyly. Bert grinned.

"I guess I can stand it," he answered.

Phin turned up next afternoon, according to appointment, and Hansel explained what was wanted, speaking of "my books" in a manner calculated to impress Phin with their number and importance, and allay any suspicion of charity, if such suspicions existed. Phin whipped out a pocket rule, set down some figures on the back of a dirty envelope, and promised to attend to it the next day.

"I suppose two coats of enamel will do?" he asked.

"I guess so," answered Hansel doubtfully. "Or maybe you'd better put on three; I'd like it nice and shiny."

"All right. Much obliged to you."

"You're welcome. Not going, are you?"

"Well, I guess you're busy and I've got some work to do in the village. Suppose I do this job to-morrow night. Would the noise disturb you?"

"Not a bit. I'd be glad to have you do it then. I—I want to have a bit of a talk with you, Dorr."

"All right, then; to-morrow night. Oh, by the way, you forgot to ask about the cost of this job."

"So I did!" exclaimed Hansel in some confusion. "How much—er—will you charge?"

"It'll be a dollar and twenty-five cents. You see, I'll have to use three brackets, and they cost quite a lot."

"Of course, and so does the board, I guess."

"Well, I get that down at the mill; they let me have lumber at wholesale prices. Good night."

Bert came in ten minutes later and at once looked at the wall over the couch. Hansel thought he seemed disappointed at finding it still bare.

There was a shake-up in the eleven that afternoon. Bert experimented with the position of left tackle, for which his weight and build admirably fitted him; but the experiment wasn't a howling success, and he went back of the line again very contentedly. Mr. Ames abducted a heavily-built youth from the first class team, and seemed fairly well pleased with the result. But, altogether, the line-up that day was a mixed-up affair, in which no one played for more than three or four minutes at a time in any one position. Even Hansel was shifted over to left end for a while, and later given a chance at left tackle. But the latter position was a new one for him, and he didn't shine in it. Everybody, the coach included, was heartily glad when the work was over for the day. Mr. Ames, Bert, and Harry went up to the gymnasium together, and, judging from the way hands were waved and heads shaken, they weren't very well satisfied with existing football conditions. Some of the team who were aware of having lately offended felt uneasy.

The next day three second team men went onto the first; among them Phipps, the quarter back. Things went better, as a result, if we except an injury to Cameron's knee which threatened to keep him out of the game for at least a week. In the ten-minute scrimmage, the first managed to score three times on the second, and there was a better exhibition of team work than at any time so far during the fall.

That night Hansel had his talk with Phineas Dorr. The latter put in an appearance at eight o'clock, armed with a six-foot white-enameled board, three iron brackets and a canvas bag of tools. The couch was moved away from the wall, and he went to work. Hansel helped him once or twice by holding up the shelf during the operations of leveling it and screwing in the first bracket. Presently he broached the subject of Cameron and the condition of Beechcroft athletics. Phin heard him through in silence, barring an occasional encouraging grunt as he worked his screwdriver. Then,

"What you say is just so, Dana," he said earnestly. "And I'm glad to find some fellow who thinks that way. It's bothered me ever since I came last fall. I've talked with some of the older fellows about it, and from what they've said, I think there's been a decline during the last five or six years in the school's ethics, so to say. I think a whole lot of the blame belongs to Johnny."

"Johnny? Oh, you mean Dr. Lambert. But I should think the principal would be the first one to—to——"

"He ought to be, but Johnny's not quite the man for the place, according to my thinking, Dana. He doesn't get close enough to the fellows. Those who don't take Greek of him don't see him sometimes for a month. Last year one of the fellows asked me what sort of a looking man he was! You see, too, athletics here are left to a committee of two members of the faculty, Ames and Foote, and three members of the two upper classes. But they very seldom get together. If any question comes up, instead of calling a meeting and discussing it and finding what's best to be done, some one goes and asks Bobby—that's Ames, you know—and Bobby says, 'All right, go ahead,' or, 'No, I don't think you'd better.' As for Johnny, I don't believe he ever saw a football game!"

"He hasn't been here very long, has he?"

"Five years. He came from the South somewhere; some small college; I think he was just an instructor in Greek and Latin. The school had been running behind for a few years, and the trustees wanted a man who would do what they told him to do, and who hadn't any very strong convictions of his own. Well, that's Dr. Lambert. Personally, I think he's not half bad. But for one thing he's too old; he's nearly sixty if he's a day; and he sticks too much to his office. He ought to get out and use his eyes, and see what's going on. I don't believe he knows that the fellows are paying Cameron's way through school; don't believe he knows who Cameron is, except for seeing his name on the books now and then. He ought to know a whole lot he doesn't. And that's why I say that I think a lot of the blame for the present lax condition of things belongs to him."

"But Mr. Ames?" asked Hansel.

"Well, Bobby's a good fellow and he means well; every fellow likes him; but I suppose he tells himself that since the principal doesn't bother his head about such affairs it isn't up to him. As for Foote, he doesn't bother himself much about anything outside his own province, which is looking after the fellows' physical condition."

"Well, who are the student members of the athletic committee?"

"Folsom and Middleton for the fourth class, and Royle for the third."

"But they're all football men!"

"Yes, that's a fact. You see, they're elected by the fellows, and the fellows generally pick out the most prominent athletes. Harry got on because he made a fine reputation as a chap with brains last year when he was assistant manager."

"I see," said Hansel thoughtfully.

"Yes, and you can see how it would be mighty hard work to keep Billy Cameron from playing football."

"Yes," said Hansel dejectedly. "Maybe I might as well chuck it. Only— no, I'm hanged if I do! There's next year yet, and if I— Look here, Dorr, I was in hope you'd join forces with me. From something Harry said——"

"What did he say?" asked Phin, working his screwdriver busily.

"That I'd better talk to you because you were—peculiar, too; he says that's what I am."

"Well, you haven't asked me yet," said Phin dryly.

"Oh! Will you?" asked Hansel eagerly.

"Yes, I will. Have you made any plans of—campaign?"

"No, I haven't. I meant to speak to Mr. Ames first; I thought he might suggest something." Phin shook his head.

"Let's leave him out of it for the present. After we've made a start we'll ask his assistance, and I think he'll give it, but just now, what with being in a bit of a pickle over the team and not wanting to lose one of his best men, it's a difficult proposition to put to him. See what I mean?"

"Yes, I see," answered Hansel. "Then what do you think we'd better do?" It seemed comforting to be able to say "we."

"I think we'd better keep next year in mind, and not count too much on this. If you and I were members of the committee, and could get Bobby to act with us on the questions that came up, we could do about as we pleased."

"Yes, but——"

"The new committee will be elected in the spring. You and I will stand."

"You might make it all right," said Hansel, "but I don't know a soul, scarcely."

"But you're going to; that's part of the conspiracy," answered Phin with a smile. "We'll begin to-morrow. I'll introduce you to the best fellows in our class, and you must set out to win them. You're certain of your place on the team, and that fact alone will carry weight. What you've got to do is to become popular, Dana."

"I don't like the sound of it," Hansel objected.

"No, I don't either. But it's in a good cause. I don't like shoving myself forward for an office, either, but it'll have to be done." Phin paused with screwdriver suspended in mid-air. "Come to think of it," he said, "there's going to be a meeting of the school next Saturday night to elect a new assistant manager of the football team; Bliss didn't come back this fall. I wonder—" He stopped and pondered a moment. "I can't really afford the time, but—I'll do it; I'll stand for the assistant managership."

"You will?" cried Hansel. "That'll be great. If you do that you'll be manager next year and——"

"And you'll be captain," said Phin quietly.

"Captain!"

"Why not? Just keep from being injured and laid off the team, that's all you'll have to do. You're a star player, and the fellows on the team like you already."

Hansel flushed.

"It isn't likely they'd elect me, though," he objected. "There's Royle, who has been here for two years already, and Cotton——"

"He graduates."

"And Conly."

"So does he. As for Royle, well, he might push you, but if we go at it right I guess we can get you in."

"I don't like it," said Hansel again.

"No, but you will have to put up with it," answered the other with a smile. "Mind, I don't ask you to swipe. All you need to do is to be friendly with the fellows, play the game the best you can, and let me manage your campaign. With you captain and me manager, I guess I can name two members of the next committee. Besides, maybe we can run our own man for the third position. I'll call to-morrow night and we'll make a few visits on some of the fellows. Meanwhile whenever we see a chance to drive in a wedge we'll do it. But I don't believe we'd best throw down the gauntlet just yet; we wouldn't gain much by worrying Bobby or antagonizing Bert and Harry."

"'Play the game the best you can, and let me manage your campaign.'"

"I think we could win Harry over," said Hansel thoughtfully.

"Maybe; we'll think about it." Phin gave a final turn of his screwdriver and stood off to examine the result. "There," he said, "I guess that finishes it for now."

"I'm awfully much obliged. It looks fine, doesn't it? I think I might as well pay you now."

"Just as you like," answered Phin, packing up his few tools.

"How much did you say it would be?" asked Hansel.

"I said about a dollar, but it will be seventy-eight cents."

"That seems awfully little," said Hansel.

"It's just right. The board was thirty cents, the three brackets and screws thirty-eight, and the enamel ten; seventy-eight in all."

"But you're not making anything!"

"No," answered Phin with a peculiar smile, "not on this job, Dana."

"But—but I wouldn't have asked you if—if——"

"That's just it, Dana," Phin replied quietly. "I guessed as much, and I don't like charity." Hansel colored up.

"I beg your pardon," he muttered.

"That's all right," answered Phin. "Good night."

"Good night," murmured Hansel.

CHAPTER VII
THE FIRST SKIRMISH

Phin was as good as his word. He was on hand the next evening at a little before eight, and he and Hansel set out to pay visits. The campaign had begun.

Phin did not make the mistake of letting his friends know that he was "rushing" Hansel, but, on the contrary, allowed them to think that he and Hansel had been going by and had just dropped in for a moment. Everybody was glad to see Phin; a few seemed genuinely glad to meet his companion; but for the most part Hansel was received "on suspicion," as he put it to himself, and given plainly to understand that were he not vouched for by Phin he would be quite unwelcome. But Hansel had the tact to take no notice of such attitudes, did more listening than talking, was modest on the subject of his football prowess and so, in every case, created a good opinion, and was directly or indirectly invited to come again. And Phin impressed upon him the necessity of accepting the invitations. After they had left the eighth study at shortly before ten, Phin accompanied Hansel back to 22 Prince, and, seating himself at the table, drew up a list of the fellows whom Hansel had met, and set down after each address a day of the week.

"That's your calling list, Dana," he said. "Better drop in in the evenings as a rule; in that way you're likely to meet other fellows."

"Talk about swiping!" groaned Hansel.

"It isn't swiping," answered Phin. "You're not after anything for yourself. It's diplomacy, that's what it is. Now you put that list where no one but you will ever see it. To-morrow night we'll try a few other visits."

Hansel sighed, and Phin smiled at his dejection.

"Cheer up! To-morrow ought to finish the calls, if we have luck and find fellows in. And, by the way, have you ever tried debating? No? Well, you'd better begin. I'll put your name up for the Cicero Society; it meets in Academy Six, every first and third Friday."

Hansel murmured his thanks confusedly, and the door crashed open in front of Bert and Harry. There was a very pleasant half hour of talk after that, and when Harry and Phin had taken their departures, the roommates continued the conversation in unaccustomed friendliness.

The mass meeting called for the election of an assistant football manager to take the place of the one who had held the office, but had not returned to the academy, was not very largely attended. Few fellows cared a button who was assistant manager, and those who did show up were there more in the hope of being able to create a little "rough house" than from any laudable desire to select a good incumbent for the office. Custom prescribed that the manager should be chosen from the fourth class, and the assistant manager from the third. Field, the fourth class president, presided. After calling the meeting to order—a not wholly successful operation, owing to a group of unsympathetic fellows at the back of the hall—he stated the business in hand and called for nominations. And he got them. Every famous man from Adam to the President of the United States was placed in nomination, and it was not until Field threatened to adjourn the meeting, and Harry had begged the audience to "cut it out," that order was sufficiently restored to allow of serious business. The names of three candidates were then proposed. One of the number arose precipitately and aroused merriment by indignantly refusing to run. Then Bert proposed the name of Phin Dorr, and there was a burst of applause. The remaining candidates begged to be allowed to retire in Phin's favor, and the voting was merely a form. Phineas Dorr was unanimously elected assistant manager of the Beechcroft Football Team. He accepted the honor in a few words which everybody applauded wildly and sat down. Whereupon Harry rapped for attention and announced to the backs of the departing audience that there would be a mass meeting at the same time and place on the following Saturday night to raise money for the support of the football team. This announcement was hailed with a few groans, and Field requested Harry to move adjournment. Hansel awaited Phin at the door and, in the innocence of his heart, congratulated him. Phin smiled grimly.

"Much obliged," he said. "I guess you don't know what a lot of hard work and how little glory goes with the office. You couldn't get any fellow to take it if it didn't lead to the managership."

"Oh!" said Hansel. "But aren't you pretty busy already?"

"Yes," answered Phin, smiling grimly. "This means that I'll have to change my getting-up hour from six to five."

Before the mass meeting took place several things of moment occurred. Hansel received notice of his election to the Cicero Society and of the fact that by paying a dollar to the treasurer he could become the possessor of a printed certificate of membership. On Wednesday the team journeyed to Parkham and defeated the local team 23 to 0. On Saturday the State Agricultural School descended upon Bevan Hills, and for thirty minutes of actual playing time kept every Beechcroft student's heart in his mouth. But in the end the visitors were forced to return home without scoring, while the academy team had five points to its credit. Hansel made numerous calls on his new acquaintances and rapidly enlarged his circle of friends. But, after all, the most important event, judged in the light of subsequent results, was the appearance on Thursday morning at a French recitation of Harry Folsom in a white sweater. Not that the color of the garment had anything to do with the matter; had it been red or green or purple the outcome would have been the same.

Mr. Ames had issued an edict at the beginning of the year to the effect that students attending his classes must be suitably dressed. In short, sweaters as features of class-room attire were prohibited. That is why when on this particular morning Mr. Ames espied Harry with a white turtle-neck sweater under his jacket he remonstrated.

"Folsom," he observed, "I've told the class that I would not permit them to wear sweaters. There is no occasion for it. You have plenty of time in the morning to dress properly. This is a French recitation; not a football game. I shall have to insist that you go to your room and take that off. And as I can't have students coming in after recitations are under way, you need not return. I shall put you down as absent."

Harry, amid the broad smiles of the others, took himself out with his offensive white sweater and *Le Cid* held the boards. Had the affair ended there this story would have been quite different, Phin and Hansel would not have thrown down the gauge of battle, and many other things would not have happened. But Harry didn't like the thought of the ridicule which would probably follow the incident and told himself that "Bobby was too blamed fussy." In the act of removing the obnoxious white sweater a beautiful idea came to him, and his face, which since leaving the class room had been clouded with annoyance, suddenly wreathed itself in a radiant smile.

An hour and a half later Mr. Ames held a recitation in German in the same room, Academy Two. With a few exceptions the same students attended as attended the French recitation. The class were assembled and in their places and the hands of the clock pointed to one minute of the hour when the door opened before a belated student. Mr. Ames, in the act of opening his book, looked down the room. The expression on his face instantly caused a unanimous turning of heads. Down the aisle walked Harry, an expression of blissful unconsciousness on his features. The white sweater was gone. In place of his former attire was an immaculate suit of evening dress. Patent-leather pumps clad his feet, the tails of his coat waved jauntily, a white vest framed a dazzling expanse of shirt bosom, from which two pearl studs peeped coyly forth, his collar and white lawn tie were in quite the best of taste, his hands were chastely hid by pearl-colored gloves, and his hair was sleek and shining. He took his seat gracefully and viewed the convulsed countenances of his class mates with an expression of courteous surprise. That expression was the last straw. Such a roar of laughter went up as never before had been heard in those sacred precincts. And Mr. Ames, after a brief struggle for composure, joined his voice to the others. Only Harry remained composed, and the look of well-bred bewilderment grew and grew. At last Mr. Ames conquered his amusement and coughed suggestively. The room quieted down.

"In place of his former attire was an immaculate suit of evening dress."

"Folsom," he remarked, "you have gone to unnecessary extremes in complying with my request, but I am glad that you appreciate my point of view. Allow me to compliment you on your appearance. I assure you you look much more respectable than at our last meeting."

Harry bowed respectfully and work began. But all during the recitation there were occasional choking sounds as some member of the class allowed his attention to wander from the lesson to Harry.

Now one cannot with impunity wear dancing pumps and open jacket out of doors on a bleak day in October. Harry discovered this fact the next morning. At noon he was in the hands of Dr. Gordon suffering with a nice attack of grippe. And that is why when, the following evening, the mass meeting was called to order, the duty of stating the purpose of the meeting fell, in the absence of the manager, to the assistant manager, which was one of the first important results hinging upon the wearing of a white sweater.

There was a full attendance, as was usually the case when there were speeches announced. After Phin had stated briefly the object of the meeting Mr. Ames arose, was cheered loudly—Field leading—and spoke of the outlook for the season. There was no good reason, he said, why, with the support of the school to count on, the team should not win this year from Fairview. As for the game with Warren, they would do their best to win that also, second in importance as it was to the final contest, but it was possible that they would have to save themselves for the greater game, as this year a lack of good new material put more work on the old men. However, they would do the best they knew how in each case, and he hoped the school would be back of them on each occasion, and let them know it.

Mr. Foote had a few words to say which no one paid much attention to—except the fellows on the platform, who had to appear polite. Then it was Phin's turn again. After a welcoming cheer had died away, he announced the enforced absence of the manager, and begged the indulgence of the audience for his inexperience. The audience was becoming waked up by that time—there is nothing like cheering to start the enthusiasm—and there were cries of "You're all right, Phin!" "Speak out, Phin!" "Don't be coy!" Hansel, sitting with other members of the team in the front row, thought Phin looked unusually serious. It couldn't be on account of nervousness, Hansel said to himself, for Phin was quite used to talking in public; and the steady, untroubled gaze of his hazel eyes proved that supposition false.

"Last year," said Phin, "we raised five hundred and forty-three dollars and seventy-five cents at the mass meeting. It was a good sum, and it carried the team through the season and left a small balance on the right side. This balance has, however, been already expended and the management has been obliged to go somewhat into debt. I am informed that a larger sum will be necessary this year. Before asking for it I am going to read to you the manager's report for last year, in order that you will know in what manner the money you gave has been used."

There were signs of uneasiness on the part of several of the fellows, and Bert strove to catch Phin's eye. But Phin didn't look in his direction as he took the sheet of paper from his pocket and spread it open. The report wasn't especially exciting; so much for football paraphernalia; so much for maintenance of the gridiron; so much for traveling expenses; and so on. At the beginning of the present season there had been left on hand ninety-three dollars and forty cents.

"Of this sum," continued Phin calmly, "thirty dollars and forty cents has gone for footballs, repairs on the tackling machine, and incidental expenses. The sum of sixty dollars has gone——"

"Mr. Chairman!" Bert was on his feet claiming attention.

"Mr. Middleton!" said the chairman.

"It doesn't seem to me that this sort of thing is interesting. We are here for the purpose of raising funds for the team, and I think we ought to go ahead and do it. There are quite a number of us who have other engagements this evening and want to get away. Besides, it has not been the custom heretofore to go into uninteresting facts regarding the accounts. Nobody, I'm sure, doubts the trustworthiness of the manager. I move that we proceed to business."

"Does Mr. Dorr insist on finishing the report?" asked Field.

"Not if the meeting doesn't care to listen to it," answered Phin suggestively.

"Mr. Chairman!" called a voice from the body of the hall.

"Mr. Spring!" answered the chairman.

"I just want to say that it seems to me that the fellows who give the money have a right to hear how it has been spent. I don't think it's a question of doubting anyone's trustworthiness; the report ought to be made public as a—a matter of principle."

This statement elicited quite a little applause.

"Do you still object, Mr. Middleton?" asked Field.

"No," answered Bert, making the best of it; "if anyone wants to hear the stuff, why, let them, by all means."

When the laughter had subsided, Phin went calmly on.

"I am about through, anyhow," he said. "The remaining sum of sixty dollars was spent for 'team expenses.'" There was an audible sigh of relief from Bert, and even Mr. Ames looked more cheerful. Hansel, who for the last few moments had been aware of something in Phin's manner and expression that was unusual, looked up in time to catch a quick, meaning glance from the speaker. For an instant he was puzzled; Phin expected something of him, but what? Then suddenly it came to him in a flash that the battle had begun, that Phin had thrown down the gauntlet, and he was on his feet, claiming recognition. He got it, and——

"I should like to ask what is meant by 'team expenses,'" he said. "All expenses are team expenses, are they not?"

"Shut up, you fool!" hissed Bert.

"The expenses in question," began Phin promptly, "are——"

"I object!" cried Bert, leaping to his feet and viewing Phin threateningly.

"I don't think the question need be answered," said Field. "It is somewhat—er—irregular."

"We want to know!" cried a voice from the back of the hall.

"You bet we do!" said another.

Field rapped for order.

"If Mr. Dorr has finished I think it would be well to——"

"Mr. Chairman," interrupted the troublesome Spring, the editor in chief of *The Record*, the school monthly, "Mr. Chairman, I move you that the assistant manager explain what is meant in this case by 'team expenses.'"

"Second the motion!" said another voice.

"It is moved and seconded," said Field wearily, "that Mr. Dorr explain the meaning. Those in favor of the motion will say 'Aye.'"

There was a loud chorus of "Ayes."

"Contrary minded, 'No.'"

Followed a deafening shout of dissent from the front rows.

"The No's appear to have it," said Field. "The motion is——"

"Mr. Chairman!"

"Mr.—er—Dana!"

"I move that a standing vote be taken."

"Seconded!" "Stand up!" "That's the stuff!" These cries from the seat of opposition at the back of the hall.

Field hesitated. Bert was scowling blackly. Cameron, to whom the proceedings might naturally have been of interest, was apparently unconcerned. Hansel wondered whether he understood what was coming. Then a standing vote was taken and almost every fellow voted in the affirmative. Field was forced to give in.

"It is moved and carried," he announced shortly, "that the assistant manager explain more fully."

Phin, who during the proceedings had kept his place at the front of the stage and awaited calmly the outcome, bowed.

"The words 'team expenses' are used in this particular case," he explained dryly, "to mean the fall term tuition of one of the members of the team."

The announcement caused a sudden commotion of audible remarks, whisperings and whistling. Those, and they were greatly in the minority, who knew who the member of the team was craned their heads for a sight of the untroubled countenance of the star half back. Bert's face looked like a thunder cloud as he scowled alternately at Hansel and Phin. Mr. Ames was studying his hands.

"Mr. Chairman!" It was Spring again. "Mr. Chairman, I'd like to ask whether it was understood that the money collected for the team was to be used to pay the tuition expenses of one of the students."

This demand was loudly applauded. Field looked toward Phin.

"I believe," answered the latter, "that there was a tacit understanding to that effect. Of course, it would not do for the school to have it publicly known that we pay a player's expenses in order to strengthen our team. But we did it last year, and if the collection is sufficiently generous to-night we shall do it again. I may add that unless we do it we shall possibly lose one of our best players."

Spring again demanded recognition and got it from the bored chairman.

"I want to say," declared Spring warmly, "that I, for one, knew nothing about it. And I dare say there are a good many others who gave money for the support of the team who are in the same fix."

"You bet!" "Oh, cut it out!" "Sit down!"

"And what's more," continued Spring defiantly, "I don't think we should be called on to give money for such a purpose. If we can't win without buying players——!"

But the rest of his remarks were lost in the subsequent uproar. A dozen fellows were on their feet, clamoring for recognition. The chairman recognized Larry Royle.

"Spring is making a big fuss about nothing," said the center. "What if we do pay Bil—pay one of the players' tuition? He's a good man and we need him; and he's cheap at the price. It seems to me that one hundred and fifty dollars is a small price to pay for a victory over Fairview. And any fellow who doesn't think that way about it had better keep his old money in his pocket!"

He sat down amid enthusiastic applause from the football men and some others. Spring struggled for Field's eye, but the latter refused to see him. Finally he subsided and immediately became the center of an excited group. Field nodded toward Phin.

"I think that's all I have to say," said the latter, his voice almost drowned by the hubbub. "It only remains for me to remind you fellows that the team can't hope for victory unless it is well supported. It needs both money and the hearty coöperation of every fellow in the school. But to-night it is money we are looking for. We ought to have about six hundred and fifty dollars to see us through the season, and I feel sure that with the spirit of the school what it is at present, we will receive from you all we deserve. I thank you."

Phin retired to his seat, viewed suspiciously by the football crowd to whom his speech had sounded, at the best, rather ambiguous. Pencils and slips of paper were in readiness and in a jiffy they were being passed about the hall. Hansel stole a look at Phin. The assistant manager was whispering calmly to Mr. Foote, who, during the excitement, had looked on affably and uninterestedly. As for Hansel, he felt rather excited. The struggle had begun, and from present indications they had won the first engagement. When the slip was handed to him he found himself in a quandary. Every fellow was expected to give as much as he could afford. Hansel felt that he could afford five dollars, since so far his incidental expenses had been very light, but if he did so, he would be defeating in a measure his own end, which was to drive Cameron off the team. If sufficient money was not pledged to-night, or secured subsequently, to pay the rest of Cameron's tuition, he thought, that youth would have to leave school. Finally he compromised on two dollars and a half, and signed his promise for that amount. Five minutes later the slips were all returned, and Phin, Mr. Ames, and Mr. Foote were adding up the amounts of the pledges. The meeting was breaking up, but the fellows lingered to hear the result. At last Mr. Ames arose and stepped to the front of the platform.

"I am requested to announce," he said when quiet had been secured, "that the total amount of the pledges is three hundred and eighty-eight dollars and fifty cents."

What more he had to say, if anything, was prevented by the noise of scraping chairs, shuffling feet and excited voices, indignant, laughing, triumphant as the case might be. The meeting came to an abrupt close, but the echo of it lasted for many days. Meanwhile Hansel and Phin had won the first skirmish.

CHAPTER VIII
MR. AMES STATES HIS POSITION

"Dana:—Try and drop in to see me for a few minutes between seven and eight this evening. I am asking Dorr also.

"Yours,

"AMES."

Hansel found this note in the rack the next forenoon. Coming out of Academy Three after a geometry recitation at twelve, he ran into Phin and the two walked over to Hansel's room together and discussed the events of the evening before and the meaning of Mr. Ames's summons.

"He probably sent my note to the house," said Phin thoughtfully. "I wonder whether he's for or against us. Perhaps Bert and his crowd have asked him to call us down. Well——"

"O Phin!" called a fellow across the campus. "Folsom asked me to tell you he wanted you to come up to his room this afternoon."

"All right, Billy; much obliged. Harry's probably a bit excited," continued Phin grimly. "I hope it won't make him worse."

Hansel was inclined to be elated over last evening's skirmish, but Phin rather discouraged him.

"I don't believe a fourth of the fellows cared a rap for the principle of the thing," he said. "But they liked to see a fuss and were glad of an excuse for not pledging money."

"But there was only about four hundred dollars pledged," answered Hansel. "Surely that won't be enough to pay the expenses of the team and Cameron's tuition for the rest of the year."

"No, it won't, I guess; I don't believe they'll be able to afford to hand over ninety dollars of it to him. But it doesn't help us much just at present, for Cameron's tuition is paid up to Christmas; even if he has to get out then, he can play football all he wants to meanwhile."

"That's so," said Hansel ruefully. "I had forgotten that."

"It may keep him from coming back next year, though. And that's what I had in mind when I decided to start things going last night. It didn't enter my head until after the meeting had been called to order. Then it dawned on me that here was a chance too good to waste. I was afraid you wouldn't understand what was wanted, though, when I'd read that 'team expense' item. But you did. By the way, we've got one new convert, anyway. Spring was down to see me this morning before I was through breakfast. You know he's editor of *The Record*, and he says he's going to write a hot editorial for the next issue, which comes out next week. I told him to go ahead, but I don't believe it will amount to much."

"But he seemed earnest enough last night?"

"Oh, Spring's earnest enough, but you see *The Record's* censored by the faculty, and if they don't want a thing to appear, it doesn't. And I don't believe they'd let anything very vigorous get in for fear it would hurt the reputation of the school."

"Oh, I see. Well, say, you stop here to-night and we'll go over to see Ames together. I'll be ready at seven, if you like."

"All right. And I mustn't forget to call on Harry this afternoon. I dare say he's wild about it."

But Phin found when he made his visit that he hadn't done justice to the manager's sense of humor. Harry seemed to think that it was a pretty good joke, and wasn't satisfied until Phin had told his story of the mass meeting.

"Bert was up here this forenoon," said Harry with a chuckle. "He's red-headed, frothing at the mouth. Says it was all my fault; that I shouldn't have given you the statement, that I had no business being sick, and a lot more poppycock. But, thunder! how was I to know you were going to read that statement? I thought you just wanted to have it in case somebody began asking questions. I wish I could have been there—in the back of the hall, I mean—and heard it all. Billy Cutler says Field looked just as though he was sitting on a hot stove!"

"I'm sorry if I've got you into trouble, Harry, but the chance was too good a one to let go by. And Hansel Dana——"

"Hansel Dana!" interrupted Harry with a grin. "There it is! He's at the bottom of the whole shindy. Say, that fellow's playing hob, isn't he? He'll have the whole school topsy-turvy if he keeps on! He's woozy on the subject of 'clean athletics,' 'school honor,' and all the rest of it. He's a perfect idiot, but you can't help liking him."

"You don't think that, Harry," said Phin gravely. "You know well enough that he's right."

"Right? Well, maybe he is right, but, great Scott! what's the use of raising Cain about it? Why can't he be satisfied with being right? What is it about virtue being its own reward? Besides, it's all perfectly useless; Billy Cameron's tuition is all paid for the term, and nothing on earth can stop him from playing football now!"

"We're working for next year, Harry."

"That's all right then," said the other heartily. "Go ahead; you have my blessing. I shan't be here next year. But just at present I'm manager of the old team and I don't want it beaten."

"Neither do we," said Phin quietly; "but we want it to win honestly."

"You're getting it, too," said Harry sadly. "I shall have to stop associating with you chaps; first thing I know I'll be as crazy as you are!"

"Wish you were," answered Phin smilingly. "We need help. How are you coming on, by the way?"

"Physically I am doing very well, thank you; recovering strength, appetite, and the use of my limbs; Doc says I can go out to-morrow; but I am troubled in mind, Phin; it worries me to see you becoming a victim to Hanselitis."

Hansel dropped in just before dinner time, after Phin was gone, and he, too, had to tell of last evening's proceedings. And he had to listen to very much the same remarks that had been made for Phin's benefit. But when Harry made the statement that nothing could prevent Cameron from playing football, Hansel took him up.

"You wait and see," he said oracularly.

"Sure, I'll wait and see," answered Harry cheerfully. "Maybe you'd like to bet on it, Hansel."

"I don't bet."

"All right, then I'll do the betting. If Billy doesn't play in the Fairview game I'll give you—what do you want?"

"Well," said Hansel, looking about the study, "I need a good sweater. I'll take that white one over there on the couch."

"Done! The old thing's got me into trouble enough already, and you can have it *if*— But I don't believe you'll own it."

"You wait and see."

"Get out, you old raven!" laughed Harry.

Hansel didn't much think the white sweater would ever come into his possession, himself, but there's nothing to be gained by acknowledging defeat beforehand, and, besides, he felt rather hopeful and pleased this evening. In the first place, if Phin and he had accomplished no more they had at least stirred things up, for all day long the chief subject of discussion among the students of Beechcroft Academy had been the mass meeting and the status of the star half back. And, in the second place, Hansel had suffered public martyrdom, and there's nothing like martyrdom to bolster up one's self-respect and increase one's self-importance. When he had reached the green that afternoon he had quickly noticed a difference in the attitude of the other members of the football team. It was not that they showed animosity, but they apparently viewed him distrustfully and seemed to avoid him as though he had suddenly become an outsider.

When the line-up for the short game came, Hansel found himself relegated to the position of right end on the second team. It was evident that Mr. Ames did not approve, and there followed a long discussion between him and Bert. But in the end the coach shrugged his shoulders as though persuaded, but not convinced, and Hansel went on to the second and played there all during the short practice. He was on his mettle, and the way he "made rings around Cutler," to use the popular expression, was highly pleasing to his adherents, of whom there were not a few among the audience that followed the play. Hansel knew, and every other fellow there knew, that his banishment to the scrub team was in the nature of a public disgrace as punishment for siding against Cameron. If there had been any doubt in his mind on this point, it would have been speedily dispelled when he reached his room after his visit to Harry.

"Well," asked Bert, who was getting himself ready for supper, "how do you like the scrub?"

"All right," answered Hansel calmly.

"Glad you like it. For that's where you'll probably play. We can't have fellows on the first eleven who are trying to get us beaten."

"Don't you worry about me, Bert," replied Hansel. "I can take what's coming to me. You won't hear any kicking if I stay on the second from now until I leave school."

"Well, you would stay there if I had my way," growled Bert angrily.

At a few minutes after seven Phin and Hansel knocked on the door of Mr. Ames's study on the first floor of Weeks. As soon as they were comfortably seated the coach plunged into his subject.

"I've asked you fellows around here," he said, "because I want to know just what you're up to; and I want you to tell me fairly and squarely."

Hansel looked toward Phin and the latter accepted the office of spokesman. He told Mr. Ames just what they hoped to do, why they wanted to do it, and what they had accomplished already. And the instructor heard him through without an interruption. When Phin had ended, Mr. Ames was silent for a moment. Then,

"Thanks, Dorr," he said gravely. "I'm glad to know this. And what is the sentiment of the school on the subject?"

"Divided, sir. I think most of the fellows don't care one way or the other."

"I dare say not. Dorr, there's been a big change in the spirit of the school during the time that I've been here as instructor. Five years ago Cameron couldn't have played on the team for a moment. I don't know just what or where the trouble has been, but I do know that we've been getting laxer and laxer right along as regards athletics. There have been two or three things done here during the last three years which you fellows have probably never heard of. And, by the way, what I am telling you to-night is quite between us three, if you please. I don't like this sort of thing any better than you do, and several times I have made myself unpopular by trying to correct it. But for the last two years I've been drifting along with the crowd; it's a thankless task to pull a lone oar against the current, and there hasn't been the help from—" The instructor pulled himself up abruptly. "But that's no matter. Now what I want to know is why you fellows haven't come to me before this and asked my assistance."

"Well, sir," answered Phin after a moment's hesitation, "we thought it would hardly be fair. You're coach, and, of course, you want to turn out a good team, one that will beat Fairview, and it seemed to us that to ask you to—to——"

"In short, Dorr, you and Dana thought I'd rather defeat Fairview than help you? Well, let me tell you, and you, too, Dana, that I don't give a hang who wins. This may sound strange to you, but it's a fact, nevertheless. I've watched things pretty closely for several years, and I've just about reached the conclusion that the school that wins more than a fair share of athletic contests is in a good way to slide downhill. There is nothing, it seems, so demoralizing to a school or college as a reputation for winning in football year after year. It brings a flood of undesirable material to the school and the *morale* suffers in consequence. Fellows who come here because they want to play football on a winning team aren't the fellows we want. They introduce the 'win-at-any-cost' spirit, and its that spirit, as you fellows know, that causes just the sort of trouble we're experiencing here now. 'Win at any cost' means trickery and dishonesty."

"You fellows can count on me, but you must recollect that I am in a difficult position. I can't put Cameron off the team; he would appeal to Dr. Lambert, in which case he would, I fancy, be reinstated. In fact, there is very little chance of doing away with Cameron this year. Perhaps if you succeed in changing the sentiment of the school from the present one of apathy and worse to one of opposition to unfair methods in athletics, you will have done enough for this year. In fact, you've got to begin at the bottom and lay your foundation; once establish a principle of athletic purity and fellows like Cameron won't trouble you. It isn't Cameron that's to blame, but the spirit of the school."

"We know that, sir," said Hansel. "I wish we didn't have to interfere with him; he's so—such a good sort, I think."

"He is," said the coach heartily. "He's one of the best-hearted chaps here. I don't believe he would willingly hurt a fly; but for all that he isn't capable of seeing anything out of the way in his position here. He would probably be highly indignant were you to suggest to him that his presence on the team was not quite square."

"Speaking of beginning at the bottom, Mr. Ames," said Hansel. "I was talking to Folsom the other day, and he said he thought the trouble was with the colleges; that they weren't strict, and that the schools naturally copied their methods."

"There's something in that," answered the instructor, "but not a great deal. I don't think the college's example influences the school very much. What does harm, however, is the frantic hunt for material at the school on the part of the college captain, or coach, or trainer. That's something that ought to be stopped. The competition becomes so keen when a good athlete is at stake that if the good athlete has a tendency toward crookedness he can get most anything he wants. I don't mean that he can command a salary, but he can secure the equivalent in scholarships, or employment at wages out of all proportion to the services."

"That's so," said Phin. "And I think there must be more in Harry's theory of example than you think. Aren't we doing just about the same thing for Cameron?"

"Well, that's a fact, but I'm not willing to lay the blame on the colleges," answered Mr. Ames. "The incongruous feature of it is," he continued, "that the fellows who connive at such things are usually fellows who would spurn the suggestion of a dishonest action. It's a case of distorted point of view, I fancy. Now, as I say, I can't take the law into my hands and disqualify

Cameron on the grounds we've discussed, but if you can work school opinion around so that there will be a demand for his removal, I'll do my part. I'd hate to have to hurt Cameron, but I wouldn't let personal liking or team success interfere."

"I'm afraid school opinion can't be altered in a moment," said Phin.

"Perhaps not, but why not ask a few of the most prominent and influential fellows to meet some evening, put the case before them and see what they think about it? If there was sufficient support pledged, you might call a mass meeting to take action on the subject; even if you lost, you would have made a stride in the right direction; the more you make the fellows think about the question the nearer you must be to your goal, for any fellow who considers the thing fairly will have to acknowledge that it's all wrong."

"Thank you, sir," said Phin. "That seems a good idea. Would you attend the first meeting?"

Mr. Ames hesitated.

"It may look to you like cowardice, Dorr," he said finally, "but I'd rather not. It seems to me that I ought to preserve neutrality as far as is possible. Besides, I don't think it would be wise to bring the faculty element into such a meeting; you fellows could do more on your own initiative."

"Very well, sir, we'll try it."

"And I wish you luck," said Mr. Ames as the boys arose. "Come around whenever you can and report progress. And whatever I can do for you I will. Oh, by the way, I wouldn't expect too much of that editorial in *The Record*; it's just possible the faculty will think it, too—er—strong. You understand? Good night!"

The meeting was duly called and met in Spring's study, in Weeks. The attendance was not encouragingly large; out of twenty-eight fellows invited by Phin, thirteen appeared. Phin, Hansel, and Spring all spoke. It was difficult at first for the audience to eliminate the personal element from the matter, and the general sentiment seemed to be that "it was hard lines on Billy Cameron." Ultimately, however, most of them consented to look at the subject from an abstract point of view, after Phin and Hansel had assured them time and again that there was nothing against Cameron personally, and that it was the principle of the thing they were concerned with. When the meeting broke up there were six certain converts, most of them fellows whose names carried weight, and some of the others had consented to "think it over"; these latter promised in any event to attend the mass meeting which, it was decided, was to be called for the following Saturday night. On the whole, Hansel and Phin were encouraged.

Meanwhile the former had been reinstated on the first team. The powers, represented by Bert, came to the conclusion that two days of disgrace was all that could be afforded, owing to the fact that there was no one who could fill the culprit's place at right end. Hansel went cheerfully back to his position and, as always, played as hard as he knew how. Cameron, who had been laid off because of injuries received in practice, was back again once more at right half, and got into things in a way which showed that his enforced idleness had done him good. The team as a whole was coming fast now, and there was hope among the more sanguine of a victory over Warren. The game with Warren school was not considered nearly so important as the contest with Fairview, and, coming as it did only two weeks before the final contest, it frequently happened that the game was purposely sacrificed in order to spare the light blue players for the supreme conflict. But for all that the Warren game was worth winning, and a decisive victory for Beechcroft was considered conclusive proof of the team's ability to cope with Fairview. This year the wearers of the light blue were in unusually good physical condition, were well advanced and, it was understood, would enter the Warren game with a determination to win. That game was not quite two weeks distant.

CHAPTER IX
THE SECOND SKIRMISH

There was a second meeting called about this time to raise additional funds for the support of the football team. The sum already subscribed was not enough for the traveling expenses, guarantees to visiting teams and clothing, and where the ninety dollars to pay Billy Cameron's tuition for the winter and spring terms was coming from was causing Harry Folsom a good deal of bother. And when the meeting had assembled he said as much. There was a very slim attendance, and a spirit of levity prevailed. Phin and Hansel were there, as was Spring, but they took no part in the proceedings, greatly, I think, to Harry's relief. The football men were conspicuously absent.

"You fellows want a good team," said Harry, "and you want it to lick everything that comes along. But you aren't willing, it seems, to pay for it. You've pledged three hundred and eighty-eight dollars, and that isn't nearly enough, and you know it as well as we do. We need at least two hundred and fifty dollars more. Last year we managed to scrape along on about four hundred and fifty dollars, but we were able to do it because the field had been put in fine shape the year before, and we didn't have that to pay for. But this fall, as anyone knows who has been down there, there's a lot of work got to be done; the place is in bad shape. The Fairview game is played here this fall, and we've got to have the field fixed up and the stands attended to. It has been estimated that it will take over a hundred dollars to put the stands in shape for the Fairview game.

"Now we can't do that and pay traveling expenses, and pay guaranties to visiting teams on any little old three hundred and eighty-eight dollars. You fellows know that when a team comes here to play us we have to guarantee them a decent sum of money. If we don't they won't come. We don't offer big guaranties, because we've never been able to afford to; if we could do that, we could get some of the best teams in this part of the country to come here. As it is, we have to pay out from twenty to seventy-five dollars at every minor game because we can't get a decent attendance. And that soon counts up. This year we have five home games beside Fairview, and only one of those games is likely to pay for itself; that's the Warren game. Every other team that comes here goes away with a little wad of our money in their pocket.

"Then there's the item of uniforms. We aren't swell dressers here, and we don't buy the best suits on the market. But even so, a little over nine dollars is the best we can do; and the fellows supply their own sweaters. Besides these expenses which I have mentioned, maintenance of ground, traveling expenses, guaranties, clothing, there are others, such as tickets for the Fairview game, advertising in the papers and by posters, footballs, blankets, stationery, stamps, and dozens of incidental expenses. You can do a little figuring yourselves and see how much of that three hundred and eighty-eight dollars is likely to be left at the end of the season. I'll tell you one thing; there aren't going to be any dividends declared!"

"How about 'team expenses'?" called some one. There was a snicker. Harry smiled.

"Well, I didn't mention that because you fellows seem to be developing a finicky attitude of late, and I didn't want to shock you. But since you've mentioned the matter yourselves, I'll just say that there remains ninety dollars of 'team expenses' to be paid. And it's got to be paid, no matter what anyone says, for the very good reason that we have given our word that we will pay it. And a certain fellow will be in a pretty mean fix if we don't pay it. He will wonder, I guess, what the word of Ferry Hill students is worth."

There was a mild clatter of applause.

"Now, fellows," went on Harry, "we've got to have at least another two hundred and fifty. And I want you to pledge it to-night. Every one of you who hasn't given already ought to be good for five dollars. And those of you who have already given—well, we don't refuse a second contribution; we aren't fussy that way; and it won't hurt you a bit. After the Fairview game is over you'll be mighty glad and proud that you helped to bring about a victory."

"Suppose we get beaten?" piped a voice from the back of the hall where the younger and more mischievous youths were congregated.

"We won't!" declared Harry promptly. "I tell you what I'll do, fellows; if you'll make up the sum to six hundred and fifty dollars, I'll guarantee that we'll lick Fairview! There! That's fair, isn't it?"

"A fair view of the situation, Mr. Manager!" called a voice. Harry joined in the laugh that went up.

"I'm not joking, fellows," he continued. "I mean what I say. Here's your chance now; a victory over Fairview for the small sum of six hundred and fifty dollars! Doesn't that strike you as cheap?"

"What security?" asked a boy down front.

"My word!" answered Harry boldly. "That's good, isn't it?"

"You bet it is, Harry!"

Phin and Hansel joined in the applause and laughter.

"All right, then," said Harry. "Now I'm going to send the slips around. Any fellow who hasn't got a pencil can get one if he will speak up. And if any of you can't write I'll do it for you, and you'll only have to make your mark. I'm going to ask—" Harry's eyes traveled about the hall and at last rested, with a twinkle, on Hansel and Phin. "I'm going to ask the assistant manager, Phin Dorr, and the best end Ferry Hill has had for many a day, Hansel Dana, to pass the slips."

There was a clapping of hands and some laughter at Harry's announcement. Phin and Hansel viewed each other questioningly.

"I'm not going to do it," whispered Hansel. But he chanced to catch sight of Harry's quizzical look and changed his mind. Phin was already crowding his way along the row of chairs. Hansel accepted Harry's challenge and followed Phin. They took the slips of white paper and passed through the hall distributing them. Some of the youngsters near the door showed a disposition to retire from the scene, but a few words from Harry brought them back.

"I'd like to say," he remarked dryly, "that neither Dorr nor Dana has time to follow you fellows to your rooms, and so if you'll kindly keep your seats you will be rendering valuable assistance."

The slips were collected and returned to the platform. Phin helped Harry count up the amounts, and the meeting broke up, although most of those present waited to hear the result.

"I hope they don't get it," said Spring to Hansel. "And I don't believe they will. I want the team to have all the money it can use, but I don't like the idea of paying Cameron's tuition out of the fund. I'm with you fellows there, Dana, good and hard."

"The trouble is, though," answered Hansel, "that they've already paid his fall tuition, and he's bound to stay and play football this season."

"Yes, but there's another year coming, and if Cameron doesn't get his tuition paid for the rest of this year, he's not going to stay here. That's certain."

"The amount pledged this evening," announced Harry, "is seventy-four dollars. It isn't enough, and I'm disappointed in you fellows. But I've told you how things stand and it's up to you." He paused, seemed about to continue, evidently thought better of it, and turned to Phin.

"Will you move adjournment?" he asked.

Phin was a pretty busy fellow these days. He got out of bed every morning at five o'clock and attended to five furnaces, in as many different houses throughout the village. By seven he was back home for breakfast, and after that meal he attended to a few chores about the house. At eight he had his first recitation, and from that time on was busy with lessons, either studying or reciting, until two o'clock, save for an hour at noon, and two days a week had recitations at three. From half-past three to five he was on the football field attending to his duties as assistant manager. And yet, in spite of all this, he found moments now and then to do odd jobs for the villagers or students. It was no uncommon sight to see Phin beating a carpet in some one's back yard long after it was too dark to see the stick he wielded. He had all the work he could attend to, for there was nothing he could not do, and his personality pleased his patrons so much that one customer led to others. He mended fences, fitted keys, whitewashed walls, now and then tried his hand at a small job of painting, cleaned yards, and had soon grown into a village necessity, without whom the housewives would have been at their wits' end. But no matter how much work was called for, Phin couldn't neglect his school duties, for he was trying for a scholarship, and on his success depended his continuance at Beechcroft. Harry tried to get him to put up a shelf for him, but Phin, scenting charity, refused to do it.

"You don't need a shelf," he declared. "It would spoil the looks of your wall. But if you insist, I'll put it up for you the first chance I have, and take just what the materials cost."

"You're a suspicious dub," said Harry sorrowfully. "I've been pining for a shelf over there for years and years, but if you choose to assign base motives to my request, I shall continue to go shelfless. I won't take favors from a chap who accuses me of duplicity."

The intimacy between Phin and Hansel grew with every passing day. Hansel was grateful for the friendship, for matters in 22 Prince weren't in very good shape those days. He and Bert passed the time of day, as the saying is, and that was about all. As for the new friends and acquaintances which Hansel had made through Phin, he cultivated them carefully, and found pleasure in so doing, but as he was beginning to be looked upon as "queer," or, as Harry put it, "peculiar," those friends didn't turn into chums. Phin and Harry were his warmest friends, and that Phin finally led in his affections was probably because of the bond of interest existing between them in the form of what Harry called the "crusade."

"He was beginning to be looked upon as 'queer.'"

CHAPTER X
HANSEL LEAVES THE TEAM

The mass meeting was surprisingly well attended. Ever since the similar assembly at which the "team expenses" item had been brought to light there had been rumors of all sorts flying about the school. It was said that Billy Cameron was not going to be allowed to play; that some of the fellows were going to demand the resignation of the present manager, and that Phin Dorr wanted the office; that the faculty was frightened lest the facts about Cameron should get into the papers; that Bert Middleton and Dana didn't speak to each other; and much more besides. All this had the effect of whetting public curiosity, and so filling the hall from platform to doors. Field had refused to preside and the honor fell to Cupples, president of the third class. After calling the meeting to order, for once not a difficult task, since the audience was consumed with curiosity, Cupples introduced Phin. Phin made the best speech of his school career that evening, but I'm not going to bore you with it, nor with the remarks made by Spring, who followed him; nor with what Hansel had to say.

The latter was rather nervous at first and had to stand some "jollying," but he soon recovered his composure and his voice, and spoke very well indeed, his earnestness impressing even the scoffers. There were plenty of these; Bert was there, and Larry Royle, and King, and Conly and others of the first team; and there was a liberal sprinkling of first class urchins, whose mission seemed to be to make as much noise and disturbance as possible. Harry was on hand, also, but he didn't scoff. "Give 'em fair play, I say," he proclaimed.

Without wishing to do any injustice to the efforts of Phin and Hansel, I think it is safe to say, that of the three speeches, that made by Spring made the most converts. Spring was terribly enthusiastic over whatever he undertook, and he had become quite wrought up over the subject which was at present disturbing the school. As a consequence he made many assertions not quite borne out by facts and, like an Irishman at a fair, hit whatever heads were within reach. This was what the fellows wanted to hear, and Spring got lots of applause, especially when he demanded to know whether the faculty was asleep, and if not, why it didn't "come to the succor of the fair name of the school, and stamp under heel this foul serpent of deceit!" (Two members of the faculty present were seen to hide their faces at this point, probably from shame.)

Of course, Phin and Hansel and Spring didn't have everything their own way. There was plenty of opposition voiced. Royle got up and made a speech that won loud applause. Royle said there were fellows in school that made him mighty tired, and that if it was the reputation and honor of the school they were bothering about, the best thing they could do was stuff pillows in their mouths.

There was a full hour of debate following the first resolution, which Hansel presented for adoption. It was too strong, and by the time it had been patched and sliced to suit the majority, it bore but slight resemblance to its first form. But that the meeting was willing to adopt any resolutions presented by them, was at once a surprise and a triumph for Phin and Hansel and Spring. As finally adopted the resolution resolved, after several "Whereases," that it was "the sentiment of the school in mass meeting assembled that Phineas Dorr, Edward Cupples, and Barnard Spring be constituted a committee to examine into the condition of athletics at the school and, at their discretion, to confer with the athletic committee and the faculty, with a view to the drawing up and adoption of a set of rules to govern athletics." This resolution went with a two-thirds vote, and the prime movers were delighted. In celebration Phin invited Hansel to dine with him the next day.

After dinner they went for a long walk together, around the lake, a matter of six miles, reaching home just as the bell on Academy Hall was ringing for vespers. Hansel told Harry about it the next day and the latter was greatly astounded.

"I never heard of any fellow dining with Phin before," he declared. "There's a popular belief here that Phin doesn't really eat, that he just lives on sawdust and shavings and other cereals."

"We had a very nice dinner," said Hansel. "Of course it was plain, and there wasn't an awful lot of it, but it was cooked finely. Mrs. Freer started to apologize once but Phin wouldn't let her. She's a dear old lady—only, I guess she isn't so very old, after all—and is mighty good to Phin; looks after him just as his own mother might. And he's nice to her, too; just as thoughtful and—er—polite as anything! They've got a nice little house there, clean and cozy and homelike. We had chicken."

"Phe-e-ew!" whistled Harry. "I'll bet they won't have it again in a year. You were a guest of honor, my boy. Anyone has only to look at Phin to know that he doesn't get a square meal once a month. If Mrs. What's-her-name is so fond of him she'd better feed him up a bit."

"I guess he doesn't pay very much," Hansel reminded.

During the walk following the dinner at Mrs. Freer's, Phin and Hansel, encouraged by success, had planned a vigorous campaign, and in the evening they called on Mr. Ames and spent nearly two hours in his study. In pursuance of their plans, Hansel, on Tuesday, four days prior to the Warren game, issued an ultimatum.

"Is Cameron going to play in Saturday's game?" he asked Bert.

"He certainly is," was the reply.

"Very well; then you'll have to count me out."

"What do you mean?" cried Bert.

"Just what I say. From now on I will not play in any outside game in which Cameron takes part."

"But—but—that'll put us in a nasty hole!" cried the other in alarm. "What sort of a way is that to act?"

"Cameron has no business on the team, and as long as he's there I'm out of it. If you like I'll keep in training and play in practice, but I won't go into the games if he is in the line-up."

I'm not going to repeat everything that Bert said; much of it he was probably quite ashamed of later; and it didn't do any good, anyway. Hansel refused to argue, refused to fight, refused to lose his temper. The matter was carried to Mr. Ames at once, but the latter decided that Hansel had a perfect right to say whether or not he would play football.

"Then I won't have him on the field," said Bert. "If he won't play against Warren and Fairview, there's no use in having him practice. We'll put Cutler in at right end and hammer some football into his thick head. But this means that we lose the Warren game, sure as fate! Hang Hansel Dana! There's been nothing but trouble ever since he came here."

"You don't think then," asked Mr. Ames, "that you could do better by dropping Cameron and keeping Dana?"

"Do you?" asked Bert moodily.

"I'm not certain. You know Warren has been playing a running game all fall, and her quarter has done some wonderful work with the ball; they say he's like a cat at working the ends. And if Fairview finds out that we're weak at right end, she'll probably try the same thing."

"I won't let Cameron go," said Bert stubbornly. "That's just what Hansel and Phin and that crowd are after, and I won't give them the satisfaction!"

"Well, think it over. I shan't interfere in the matter. Keep Cameron or Dana, whichever you think best."

The next day Hansel was not at right end on the school team, and, in fact, did not appear on the green at all. By night it was known throughout the school that Dana had been put off the team because of his anti-Cameron attitude. It did not get out until after the Warren game that he had refused to play because of Cameron's presence. The football authorities came in for a good deal of criticism, for Hansel was recognized as almost the best player on the team, and to put him off just before the Warren game seemed the height of folly. Hansel refused to talk on the subject.

On Thursday Hansel suddenly realized that he had not seen Phin for two days, a most unusual occurrence, since Phin had formed the habit of bringing his lunch to school with him, and eating it in a corner of the library while he studied, and Hansel usually dropped in there for a chat on his way back from dinner. But the library had been empty the last two days, and Phin had not shown up, either at recitations or at Hansel's room. So on Thursday afternoon Hansel set off to the village to look him up. He was glad of something to do, for since he had left the eleven the afternoons had grown interminably long and frightfully dull. As he crossed the green the fellows were just lining up for practice, and he could see Cutler at his place on the right end of the first. When he rang the bell at Mrs. Freer's it was Phin himself who opened the door. He looked paler and thinner than ever, and there were dark streaks around his eyes, as though he had not had sufficient sleep.

"Oh!" he said at sight of Hansel, "I thought it was the doctor."

"Doctor?" asked Hansel. "Are you sick?"

"No, but mother is. He said he'd be back at three and he hasn't come yet."

"Your mother?" exclaimed Hansel, dropping his voice to match Phin's quiet tones. "Is she here?"

"Did I say my mother? Well, I didn't mean to. You see— Come in a minute and I'll tell you." Hansel followed him to the little parlor. Phin went to the window for another anxious look up the street, and then came back to where Hansel stood beside the old white marble mantel. "I didn't mean to let it out, Hansel, but I don't believe it matters, anyway. I kept it secret on her account; she made me promise. She wouldn't come out here this winter unless I promised to keep it secret; you see, Hansel, she thought the fellows might—well, look down on me, I suppose, if they knew my mother did dressmaking. I told her, though, that if I attended to furnaces and beat carpets, I guessed the fellows could stand her doing sewing. But she was afraid, and so I agreed to keep it quiet. After all——"

"You mean Mrs. Freer?" asked Hansel, a light dawning on his mind. "She's your mother?"

"Yes, one of the best a fellow ever had, Hansel. She's worked like a slave for me for years. And that's the reason I wanted her to come here this year and take this house. I knew I could keep an eye on her, and see that she didn't starve herself to death in order to send me money. I thought we could rent the spare room and that she would be able to get some dressmaking to do, but it hasn't turned out very well. And now she's down sick with the grippe, and the doctor's afraid it's going to turn into pneumonia. I've been up with her three nights, Hansel, and I'm just about played out."

"I'm mighty sorry," muttered Hansel. "Look here, what can I do? Let me go and find the doctor for you? Where does he live?"

"Will you?" asked Phin eagerly. "I don't like to leave her for very long at a time. It's Dr. Gordon, you know, three blocks down, on the corner. I'll be very much obliged——"

But Hansel was already hurrying along the street. The doctor had just returned from a trip into the country when Hansel reached his house, and was already preparing to go to Mrs. Freer's. He offered to take Hansel back that far with him in the buggy, and Hansel jumped in.

"Phin says you're afraid of pneumonia," said Hansel as they rattled up the village street.

"Looks like it now, but she may fool us," was the cheerful response. "If she had enough vitality to keep a mouse alive I wouldn't worry. Look here, are you a friend of theirs?"

"Yes," answered Hansel.

"All right; then I'm not telling secrets, I guess. She's young Dorr's mother; knew that, didn't you? She married again after his father died, and from what I gather the second marriage didn't turn out very well; present husband's still alive, I believe. Fact of the matter is, they're too poor to buy decent food; they're both of 'em just about half starved. I had a dickens of a time trying to get her to take white of egg; she said eggs were very dear, and thought something else might do. The boy seems awfully fond of her, and he's nursed her right along for three days, but it seems to me he'd better leave school and find some work, so he can take care of her. Here we are. How's that? Wait to see— Oh, all right; I'll be out in ten minutes, I guess, and I'll tell you how she is."

Hansel turned up the street and walked as far as the first corner, keeping an eye on the little white gate for fear Dr. Gordon would escape him. And as he strolled along his mind was very busy. When, finally, the doctor reappeared, Hansel hurried up to him.

"Which way are you going, sir?" he asked.

"Down to the other side of town, across the railroad. Why?"

"May I go along? I'd like to speak to you."

"All right, my boy; in you go." When the buggy had turned, scraping, and was again headed toward the railroad, Dr. Gordon observed Hansel with frank interest. "You're one of the academy boys, I suppose?"

"Yes, sir."

"Well, now about Mrs. Freer. I think she's going to pull through without lung complications. It's a bit early yet to say for sure. I'm going back this evening at ten, and if you're interested enough to call me up by 'phone at about half-past, I'll tell you what there is to tell."

"Thank you, doctor," answered Hansel gratefully, "I'll do that."

"All right; call 48-3."

"Do you think she ought to have a nurse, sir?" asked Hansel presently.

"Um-m; she could use one, but I guess they can't afford it, or think they can't. The boy does pretty well—if he doesn't give out."

"Is there a nurse they could get if—if they decided they wanted one?"

"Yes, Mrs. Whitney, on Arlington Street, would be just the person for them. I don't think she's engaged just now, either."

"Thank you, sir. If you'll pull up I'll get out here, I guess."

"Oh, all right. Call me up to-night, eh? Glad to have met you. Good-by!"

Hansel hurried back to the academy and sought Harry on the green. Taking him aside he told about Phin's predicament.

"His mother!" marveled Harry with a low whistle. "Well, I'll be switched!"

"Yes, and she needs a nurse, Harry; Dr. Gordon says so; and they think they can't afford it. But, of course, she's got to have one."

"Has she?" asked Harry, trying to follow Hansel's argument. "Well, if you say so."

"We've got to get hold of some money."

"Oh, that's it? How much?"

"I don't just know, but I think nurses charge about fifteen dollars a week."

"Well, who's going to get her, you?"

"I suppose so."

"Well, hurry along then. She won't want any pay until the end of her week, and meanwhile we'll find plenty of money; lots of fellows will be only too glad to help Phin."

"But—but do you suppose he'll consent?"

"Go send the nurse there and ask consent afterwards," said Harry. "Come around this evening and we'll talk it over. Do you need any coin now?"

"No; but I have a couple of dollars in my pocket if I do. I'll be up about eight."

An hour later he was ringing Phin's doorbell again. He could hear Phin tiptoeing down the stairs, and in a moment the door was opened.

"How is she?" asked Hansel.

"Asleep now; I guess she's just about the same. The doctor, though, said he thought she was doing rather well. It was good of you to call, Hansel."

"Not at all, because— By the way, is there anything I can do for you? Any errands or anything?"

"Not unless you can study and recite for me. I guess my scholarship's a goner, Hansel."

"Nonsense! When you explain—" Phin shook his head.

"Johnnie isn't a good man to explain to," he said hopelessly. "Well, it can't be helped. After all, I dare say I'd better be at work; college can wait for a few years. But won't you come in?"

"No, I must get back. I—I just stopped in to tell you that Mrs. Whitney will be here at eight o'clock to take charge."

"Who's she?" asked Phin with wide eyes.

"Nurse, Phin. You see, the doc thought you'd better have one, and so a few of the fellows— We knew you didn't want to stand the expense, but— you can pay it back, if you want to, any time you like; it's just a sort of a loan, you know———"

Hansel ceased his embarrassed explanations, and glanced at Phin. A little smile was trembling around the latter's mouth and his eyes had a misty look that sent Hansel retreating backward down the steps.

"And so—so she'll come at eight," murmured Hansel. "Good-by!"

Then he turned and hurried through the gate and up the street, whistling a bit breathlessly, and much out of tune.

"Of course when a fellow hasn't had much sleep and gets worried like that," he explained to himself, "it's no wonder he wants to cry. I dare say I would!"

CHAPTER XI
HANSEL MAKES A BARGAIN

The principal's residence was a small two-storied brick cottage standing back of Weeks Hall, and hidden from sight by a grove of trees, through which the graveled driveway wound in and out. At half-past seven Hansel found himself standing before the front door. Its stained glass in strange shades of green, yellow, and brown added to his depression. He had never spoken to Dr. Lambert and, like most fellows, stood very much in awe of him, and his present mission was one which might not, he believed, please the doctor. A white-aproned maid admitted him to a tiny library, asked his name and disappeared. Ten minutes by the old clock in the hall passed; then footsteps sounded without, and the doctor stood at the doorway.

"This is Dana, I believe? I have the name correctly?" he asked. Hansel murmured assent.

"Come this way, please," said the principal. Hansel followed him across the hall and into the office, a plainly furnished room with unpapered walls, against which a few photographs of the school hung. The doctor motioned Hansel to a chair, seated himself at the broad-topped desk, and looked politely attentive.

The principal was a small-framed man of some fifty-five years of age, dressed habitually in a suit of smooth black cloth with a long-tailed coat. His countenance was neither repellent nor attractive, but Hansel thought it wholly lacking in sympathy, and his embarrassment grew each moment. The doctor passed his hand slowly over his drooping mustache, which, like his hair, was somewhat grizzled, and coughed softly.

"You—ah—wished to see me?" he asked finally.

"No, sir," answered Hansel, "that is, yes, sir, if you please." After this unfortunate beginning he relapsed again into embarrassed silence, casting about wildly in his mind for the right words to introduce his subject. Finally, when the expression of surprise on the principal's face had deepened to one of annoyance, Hansel took the plunge.

"It's about Phin, sir," he blurted.

"Phinsur? Who's Phinsur?" asked the doctor with a frown.

"Phin Dorr, I mean."

"Ah, yes, Dorr; hum; what about Dorr?"

"His mother's sick, sir."

"Indeed? I am very sorry to hear of it."

"And Phin has had to stay at home and look after her."

"At home? He has left the academy?"

"No, sir, he lives in the village with his mother, Mrs. Freer."

"Really? I was not aware of that."

"Nobody was, sir." And Hansel, with much floundering, explained. When he had finished, the doctor nodded gravely in token of understanding.

"A very devoted mother, Dana, but ill advised. I do not approve of parents coming here to live with their sons. May I ask what it is you want me to do?"

"Why, sir," answered Hansel, gaining confidence, "you see Phin has been obliged to be absent from recitations for two or three days, and he is trying for a scholarship, and he is afraid he won't get it on account of being absent."

"And he has asked you to intercede for him?"

"No, sir, he doesn't know I've come to see you, but he's a particular friend of mine, sir, and I don't want him to lose the scholarship. I thought if you knew why he was absent you would—would make allowances."

"So I will," answered the principal gravely. "So I will. I don't approve of the arrangement whereby Mrs.—Freer, you said?—whereby Mrs. Freer is living in the village, but that is another matter. You may tell Dorr, if you wish, that he will be given every opportunity to make up what recitations he has missed." He drew a sheet of paper toward him and wrote on it in slow, careful characters. "Dorr, I believe, is a very worthy lad, and he should be congratulated on having such devoted friends."

"Thank you, doctor," murmured Hansel. He arose, but the other motioned him back.

"While you are here," said the principal, "I should like to discuss another matter with you. I understand from Mr. Ames that you are one of the prime movers in a—ah—movement to alter the athletic arrangements here?"

"I suppose I am, sir."

"Kindly tell me what it is you wish to accomplish."

And Hansel told him, not very fluently, I fear, and the principal heard him through with unchanging countenance, his eyes from under their bushy eyebrows scrutinizing the boy's face every instant. When Hansel had finished, the doctor nodded thoughtfully once or twice.

"I begin to understand. Your position is well taken, it seems to me, but I do not very clearly understand athletics. The athlete has always seemed to me to be a—ah—privileged character, with a set of ethics quite his own. But you, I understand, apply the ethics governing ordinary affairs to him." The doctor's voice seemed slightly tinged with irony. "Am I right?"

"It seems to me," answered Hansel boldly, "that what would be dishonest in the schoolroom or in business would be equally dishonest in sport."

"Possibly, possibly," answered his host with a wave of his hand which seemed to thrust argument aside. "And this boy, Cameron, whom you mention as a specific case? You are certain that his tuition is paid by the— by his fellows?"

"Paid from the football expense fund contributed by the fellows; yes, sir."

"And that fact, in your estimation, should prohibit him from playing the game of football?"

"With other schools, sir."

"But if the—ah—other schools do not offer objections?"

"I don't suppose they know what the facts are, sir."

"I see. Then you think that if the other schools knew they would object?"

"I think so, sir; I think they would protest him."

"In which case——?"

"Why, then it would be up to—I mean, sir, that in such a case it would lay with you to say whether or not he could play."

"Thank you. You have given me quite a good deal of information on a subject of which I have been, I fear, inexcusably ignorant. I begin to think that I have been mistaken, that athletic ethics are much the same as any other. Strange, very strange!" He arose and Hansel followed his example. At the door he held out his hand. Something almost approaching a smile softened the immobile features. "Good night, Dana. I am glad to have made your acquaintance. We shall meet again, doubtless."

Outside Hansel took a deep breath of relief.

"Thunder!" he muttered with a shiver, "that's like visiting in an ice chest! I wonder, though, if he is going to take our side!"

Then he hurried off to keep his appointment with Harry.

The next afternoon, Friday, he called again at Phin's. The door was opened by a stout, placid-faced woman in a blue-striped dress and white apron.

"Good afternoon, Mrs. Whitney," said Hansel. "Is Phin in?"

"Yes, but he is asleep, I think. He didn't go to bed until about midnight, and I haven't waked him yet; he seemed to need the rest."

"Oh, well, don't call him, then. How is Mrs. Freer?"

"Much better this morning. The doctor thinks she'll soon be around again now. She had some beef tea this noon."

"That's fine." Hansel lowered his voice for fear the patient upstairs might hear. "Mrs. Whitney, some of us fellows at the school are going to pay you, so don't you take anything from Phin or his mother, if they want you to, will you? You see, they're rather short of ready money just now, and we want to help Phin out a bit."

"I understand," said the nurse, with a smile. "I'll look to you for my money."

"Yes, but don't you leave until the doctor says you may; Phin may want to send you off before it's time, you know."

"Very well, I won't pay any attention to him," said Mrs. Whitney.

"That's right. And please tell Phin, when he wakes up, that I called and wanted to see him to tell him that it's all right about the scholarship."

"About——?"

"The scholarship; he'll understand."

"Very well, I'll tell him," answered the nurse. "I hope it's good news, for the poor boy's just about worn out."

"It is," Hansel assured her. "Good-by."

The next morning Phin was back at school, and Hansel had to listen to his thanks when the two met in the library at the noon hour.

"Oh, rot!" said Hansel finally. "To hear you talk one would think I'd taken some trouble. It was the easiest thing in the world."

"Maybe," answered Phin, his pale, thin face very earnest, "but it was a mighty kind thing to do, Hansel, and I want you——"

"La-la, la-la-la, la-la!" sang Hansel, to drown the other's protestations. "Phin, you annoy me! Shut up! Who's going to win this afternoon?"

Phin smiled, shook his head, and took a generous bite of the sandwich he held in his hand. "You ought to know better than I," he replied. "I feel as though I hadn't been here for a month. What do they say?"

"Say we'll win, but I'm afraid we won't. And I feel like—like a traitor, Phin. If Warren beats us—!" He shook his head sadly.

"Heroic measures are sometimes necessary," responded Phin, with his mouth full. "Whichever way it turns out, you won't be to blame."

"I suppose not, but it's plaguey hard to see your team beaten, and know that you've helped beat it!"

And, as it turned out, that was just what Hansel had to see, for after the first fifteen minutes of play, during which Beechcroft, having secured the ball on the kick-off, advanced from her ten-yard line by steady rushes to Warren's goal line, and from there sent Bert over for a touchdown, from which Cotton kicked goal, Warren showed herself the superior of the home team. For the rest of that half she played on the defensive, and the period ended with the score 5 to 0. But of the last half there was a different tale to tell.

Beechcroft kicked off, and Warren's left half back ran the ball in thirty yards before he was finally downed on his forty-five-yard line. Then came a try at the center of the light blue, which netted a scant two feet, and the Beechcroft adherents shouted their glee. But that was almost the last opportunity they had for such shouting. On the next play the Warren quarter back reeled off twenty yards around Beechcroft's right end, and Hansel, watching from the side-line, clinched his hands and called himself names. Warren was quick to see her advantage. Time and again the right end was tried, and always for a gain until, seven minutes from the beginning of play, Warren's full back was pushed over for a touchdown. Those seven minutes comprised a fair sample of the subsequent proceedings. Cutler was taken out, and Forrester, a second team man, was put in his place. But, although Forrester did better work than his predecessor, Beechcroft's defense against end runs was woefully weak, and gain after gain was made around her right side. At the left end of her line King did good work and, although Warren's nimble quarter got around there once or twice for short gains, he had little to reproach himself with. Had the other end been as difficult for the opponent, the final score would have been different. As it was it was 17 to 6, and it was a gloomy lot of fellows that climbed the terrace after the last whistle had blown. As for Hansel, he had been in his room for fifteen minutes then; he had not had the heart to stay and watch the contest after the first score of the second half; and not for much money would he have faced at that moment the looks of the Beechcroft players. He believed himself to be in the right, only—the right looked all wrong!

At five o'clock Bert came in, gloomy and disheartened. After a glance at Hansel, who was pretending to study in the window seat, he threw down his cap and seated himself at the table. Presently Hansel heard the hurried scratching of a pen, and looked across at his roommate. Bert, cheek on hand, was writing feverishly, scowling darkly the while. The clock ticked annoyingly loud. Hansel cleared his throat, opened his mouth, closed it again, and turned back to his book. The pen scratched on and on, and the clock ticked louder than ever. Finally, with a rush of blood to his cheeks, Hansel put down his book.

"Bert," he said softly, "I'm awfully sorry."

"I dare say!" was the bitter reply.

"I am, though; I feel like a low-down mucker!"

"Well," growled Bert, "how do you suppose I feel?"

"It wasn't your fault," answered Hansel. "You played the swellest sort of a game; so did all the fellows; but I—well, maybe it wouldn't have made any difference if I had played, but I can't help——"

"Difference!" cried Bert scathingly. "It would have made the difference between a defeat and a victory! That's all the difference it would have made!"

"I'm sorry," muttered Hansel again.

"Much good it does. How do you spell resignation? Two s's or one?"

"One; r-e-s-i-g— What are you doing?" Hansel leaped from the seat and hurried across the room.

"Resigning," answered Bert gloomily.

"What? Resigning the captaincy? Bert, you're not!"

"I am though. What's the use of trying? Let 'em call me a squealer if they like! I'm through with it!"

"You shan't do it!" cried Hansel.

"Who's going to stop me?" growled Bert.

"I am! Look here, Bert, you can't do that! Think what it will mean! Who's going to take your place? It will play hob with the team; there won't be a ghost of a show to win from Fairview!"

"There isn't now," replied the other bitterly. "You're a nice one to talk that way, aren't you?"

"I can't help it," answered Hansel stubbornly. "You mustn't do it, Bert; it isn't right! It's your duty to——"

"Oh, cut it out!" flamed Bert. "Don't *you* lecture me about duty! You who didn't care enough whether we won or didn't win to stand by us when we needed you! You lost the game to-day; we didn't! Think about that a while and don't talk duty to me, or tell me what I ought or ought not to do!"

He turned again to his note, signed his name with a sputter of ink, and blotted it.

"Are you going to send that?" asked Hansel quietly.

"Yes."

"Do you know what it means?"

"Did you know when you refused to play?"

Hansel was silent. Bert folded the note, thrust it into an envelope and addressed it to Mr. Ames. Then,

"I'll make a bargain with you, Bert," said Hansel.

"What sort of a bargain?" asked the other suspiciously.

"If you won't send that I'll report for work to-morrow and I'll play, Cameron or no Cameron! What do you say?"

Bert stared a moment, and Hansel saw hope take the place of gloom on his face.

"Do you mean it?" he asked huskily.

"Yes," answered Hansel. "Here's my hand on it."

Bert took it, laughed uncertainly, rubbed a hand across his eyes and pushed back his chair. Then he tore up the note and dropped the pieces in the wastebasket.

"Let's go to dinner," he said.

CHAPTER XII
THREE IN CONSPIRACY

"And so I told him I'd go back to work to-morrow," ended Hansel somewhat sheepishly. Mr. Ames smiled.

"And all those noble resolutions of yours, Dana?" he asked with mock reproachfulness.

"I can't help it," muttered Hansel. "I—I just had to give in. If you'd seen Bert's face you'd have done the same."

"I dare say I should," answered the other seriously. "I don't blame you, Dana; and perhaps it's just as well, anyhow. From what you've told me of Dr. Lambert's remarks the other night, I gather that he has something on his mind; I wouldn't be surprised if——"

"What, sir?" asked Phin.

"Er—nothing; it was just an idea of mine. We'll wait and see. Well, two weeks from now we'll be a very jubilant or a very depressed lot here at Beechcroft."

"Who do you think will win, sir?" asked Phin.

"'Who do you think will win, sir?' asked Phin."

"With Dana and Cameron both in the game I think we should. But Fairview has got a pretty heavy lot of men, and they're fast, too, I understand. But I'm going over there Saturday to see them play, and when I get back I'll know more about them. Of course, they won't show any more than they have to, and I dare say they'll play a lot of subs, but just the same there'll be plenty to see. Look here, Dorr, why don't you come along with me? You haven't got anything special to do, have you, on Saturday? It won't cost you anything, because I've got mileage."

"I'd like to," answered Phin wistfully, "but I guess I ought to stay here and study. I've got a good deal to make up."

"Well, I need company, and I tell you what we'll do. You come along and take your books, and I'll hear you in German on the way over. And I'll hear your French that night, if you like. What do you say?"

"It's very kind of you, sir, and if they don't need me here that afternoon, I'll be glad to go."

"They won't need you. I'll tell Folsom to get along without you. The game with Parksboro won't amount to much. We're going to play second string men almost altogether, and send the first out in the country for a walk."

"Then we won't see the game?" asked Hansel.

"You can see the first half; then I want the lot of you, the ones that don't play, to mosey over to Brookfield and back, if it's a decent day. By the way, Phin, you can set your mind at rest about your studies; the doctor tells me you are to be allowed every facility for making up lost recitations. But I forget; you know about that, don't you?"

"Yes, sir, Hansel said John—I mean Dr. Lambert—was very kind, sir."

Mr. Ames grinned.

"Funny how the fellows like to call us by diminutive forms of our first names here, isn't it?" he asked. "Last year—you remember, Dorr, I guess?—Putnam, who graduated last spring, blurted out my pet name in class room. I had called him down for not knowing his lesson. 'Mr. Bobby,' he said earnestly, 'I studied two hours on that last night, sir!'"

The boys laughed.

"It's only the ones the fellows like," said Phin, "that get pet names."

"Thank you," laughed Mr. Ames. "I feel better."

"It's so, sir," protested Phin earnestly. "You never heard any of us call Mr. Foote 'Sammy,' sir."

"Come, come, Dorr, that's treason," said the instructor, shaking his head smilingly. "You're a bit hard, you chaps, on Mr. Foote." Phin made no answer.

"By the way," asked Mr. Ames, "I meant to ask after your—after Mrs. Freer. How is she getting along?"

"Very nicely, sir, thank you. It isn't a secret any longer; about her being my mother, I mean. It was her idea, sir; she got it into her head that the fellows would think it funny if they knew she earned money by dressmaking."

"She was mistaken," answered Mr. Ames quietly. "I don't think we have many snobs here, do you, Dana?"

"No, sir," Hansel replied. "Although some of the fellows who come from a few of the prominent schools seem inclined to look down a bit on the fellows who don't."

"Yes, that's so, I guess. Well, you're showing them that their schools haven't a mortgage on football, eh?"

"That's what he is," answered Phin heartily.

The next afternoon witnessed Hansel's return to his old place on the first team. He was doubtful as to the attitude the other members would show toward him, but as it turned out his doubts were unnecessary. Most of them seemed glad to see him back again, and big Royle absolutely slapped him on the back, a token of friendliness which, because of its vigorousness, was quite as disconcerting as it was unexpected. Chastened by Saturday's defeat by Warren, the team buckled down to work in a manner that was highly encouraging, and pushed the second all over the field.

The next day Hansel stole an hour between recitations, and walked to the village and paid a visit to the little book store where the students bought their stationery. As the proprietor wrapped up the half dozen blue books and the two scratch pads which had been purchased, he remarked casually:

"Well, maybe the next time you call you'll find us in our new quarters."

"Oh," said Hansel, "are you going to move?"

"Yes, they're going to tear this place down and put up a big four-story block here. My lease is up next week, and I'm going up the street to the store just this side of Perry's drug store. I expect I'll get back here when the new building's done. Well, it's time it was torn down," he added disgustedly. "The place is almost ready to fall to pieces. I haven't been able to get them to make any repairs for over a year."

Hansel paid for his purchases and went out. On the sidewalk, from sheer curiosity, he paused and examined the building that was to disappear. It was a small affair, two stories and a half high. The ground floor was taken up by the book store, and by the entrance to a stairway leading to the upper floors, the first of which was occupied by a tailor. From his windows Hansel's gaze roamed higher to the single casement under the peak of the roof, and a spot of color caught his eyes. He moved to the curb and looked up again. Yes, it was undoubtedly a light blue Beechcroft flag which he saw. Evidently, then, one of the students had quarters up there. Well, whoever he was, he'd have to move out and find a new room very shortly. Hansel started up the street, paused and turned back, struck by a thought. After a moment of indecision he returned to the store.

"Who lives on the top floor here?" he asked.

"Top floor?" answered the bookseller. "A Mrs. Wagner. She's a German woman, a widow. She works in Barker's laundry. She has three rooms upstairs, and gets them for almost nothing. Lets the front one to students and makes a pretty good thing out of it, I guess."

"Who are the students?" Hansel asked. "Do you know their names?"

"Let me see. One of them is named Sankey or Sanger, or something like that. I don't know his friend's name."

"Sanger, I guess," said Hansel. "I know there is such a chap. They'll have to move out, too, I suppose."

"Yes, we've all got to go inside of a fortnight. For my part, I'll be glad to get out of here."

"You don't happen to have heard what this Mrs. Wagner is going to do?"

"No, but I guess she'll be able to find another place, all right. I guess she isn't very particular."

"Thank you," said Hansel. He went back to the street and meditated. Then he passed in at the entrance to the upper stories and mounted the stairs. The first flight was well lighted, but when he came to the second he had to grope his way up, for the place was as dark as Egypt. From the upper corridor four doors opened, one of them, as was evident, to a closet filled with trash, and the others to the three rooms. The only light came from a small and very dusty skylight let into a leaky roof. Hansel went to the door of the room on the front of the building and knocked. There was no answer. As he had presumed, the occupants were at school. On the door were tacked two cards bearing their names. What with the poor writing and the lack of light, it was all Hansel could do to decipher them. But he succeeded at last, and learned that the names of the occupants were John Wild Sanger and Evan Fairman Shill. He had learned all that it was possible to learn at present, and so he made his way cautiously down the stairs and hurried back to the academy.

After football practice that afternoon Hansel walked back to the campus with Harry Folsom. There had been something of a slump in the team, and Harry was looking rather gloomy for him; it took a good deal to ruffle his cheerfulness. After they had discussed the cause of the slump, and had attributed it to a variety of things, and Hansel had predicted a return to form the next day, the latter brought the conversation around to the subject upon which his thoughts had been engaged ever since the forenoon.

"Say, Harry," he asked, "do you know a fellow named Sanger, who lives in the town?"

"Johnny Sanger? Sure, I do. He lives over Dole's store; rooms with a fellow named Sill."

"Shill; but that's the chap. Well, what sort of a fellow is he?"

"Sanger? Oh, he's a sort of a frost. He's in the second class, I think, and I also think that he was there last year, too. Somebody told me that his folks have lots of money, and give Johnny all he wants, and he doesn't spend any of it from the time he comes until he goes home in the spring. But I don't know much about him personally. In fact, he may be a very decent sort, after all; you can't believe all you hear."

"And who is Shill?"

"Don't know him except by sight. He's a tall and thin youth with an earnest countenance; wears glasses, I think."

"Are his folks rich, too?"

"Search me, my boy. Say, what the dickens are you after, anyhow? Take me for a city directory, do you? Or a copy of the school catalogue?"

"S-sh, don't excite yourself," laughed Hansel. "I'll tell you all about it. In fact, I want your help. Can I have a few minutes of your valuable time? Or are you going to study?"

"Don't be silly," answered Harry, leading the way up to his room. "Who ever studies with exams two months and more away? Take the Morris chair and make yourself 'ter hum.' Now, then, unburden your mind. But let me tell you before you start that I'm dead broke. If you are thinking of hiring any more nurses, old son, you mustn't ask me. And that reminds me that I haven't collected all that money yet; there are three fellows still owing me. What you ought to do, Hansel, is to start a hospital."

"It isn't a nurse this time," answered the other, "but it's Mrs. Freer again."

"The dickens it is! What are you going to do now? Buy her a new silk dress or send her to Europe?"

"Well, you quit being funny and I'll tell you."

"Oh, I'm not funny; I can't be; I try awfully hard, but I can't make it."

"Well, stop trying then. And listen here, Harry. You know how Phin and his mother are fixed; they have mighty little money; she's been trying to make some sort of a living by doing sewing and dressmaking, but Phin says she hasn't found much to do. I suppose that's only natural in a town like this. I guess most of the women do their own dressmaking, eh?"

"Can't say for sure," answered Harry with a broad smile, "but judging by some of the dresses you see, I dare say you're right."

"Well, anyway, they're having a hard pull of it. You know how Phin works; he gets up before it's light and he works until long after it's dark, and I don't suppose he makes very much, either. It's a shame!"

"Sure it is! But we can't support them, Hansel. I like Phin as much as you do, and I've got a lot of respect for that mother of his; she's a dandy sort of a mother to have; but—well, what the dickens can we do?"

"Help them," answered Hansel promptly.

"Well—but how?" asked Harry dubiously.

"You know they've got a room at their house that they want to rent. I've seen it, and it's a dandy. If they had rented that when school began they'd have been all right, Phin says. It's only three dollars a week, but I suppose that three dollars means a whole lot to them."

"I suppose so. What then, O Solomon?"

"Well, I propose to find some one to take it for the rest of the year."

"Oh! It sounds simple, but can you do it?"

"I think so, if you help me."

"Here's where I come in, eh? What do you want me to do? Walk through the town with a placard on my back? Go around with a dinner bell yelling 'Oyez! Oyez! Oyez! There is a fine room for rent at Mrs. Freer's, and the price be moderate?'"

"No, I want you to hush up and let me do the talking for a minute," Hansel laughed. Harry looked hurt.

"Let you do the talking!" he muttered. "You don't seem to realize the fact that you've been talking a steady stream ever since you entered my humble apartment."

"I was in Dole's this morning," said Hansel, "and he told me that he had to move out inside of a fortnight, because the owner is going to pull that old building down and put up a big four-story affair."

"Phew!" whistled Harry. "Won't that be swell? Think of Bevan Hills with a four-story block! Maybe there'll be a real store there when they get it finished!"

"Well, do you see what I'm driving at?" asked Hansel.

"Driving—no, I'm blessed if I do!"

"Didn't you just tell me awhile ago that this fellow Sanger lives over Dole's store?"

"Yes, but——"

"Well, do you think he's going to stay there after they pull the place down?"

"Of course not, you idiot, but what's that got to do with Mrs. Freer's room that she wants to—" Harry paused. "Look here, you don't mean that you're thinking of trying to rent Mrs. Freer's room to Sanger and Sill, or Shill, or whatever his silly name is?"

"Why not?"

"But supposing he doesn't want to go there?"

"I intend to make him."

"Oh, yes, indeed! Go ahead and rave, poor youth! Only, after a while, kindly make an effort and talk sense!"

"Well, why shouldn't those fellows take that room? It's a good one, and it isn't nearly as far from school as the one they're in now. Besides, it's cheap."

"It's three dollars, and I'll bet they haven't been paying more than two where they are."

"But if Sanger's folks are well off, there's no reason why he shouldn't be willing to pay three, is there?"

"No, only maybe he'd rather not," Harry answered dryly. "If what I've heard of Johnny Sanger is true, he'd much rather save that dollar than spend it. So it seems likely that what he will do when he gets turned out of his present quarters is to hunt around the town until he finds something nice and cheap."

"All right, but suppose he can't find anything?"

"What's the good of supposing that? Aren't there lots of rooms to be had?"

"I don't believe so; at least, not at this time of year. You know there aren't many more rooms in the fall than will accommodate the fellows who want to live in town. I heard Spring talking about it when I first came here. He said that if the school kept on growing, they'd either have to build a new dormitory or put up some more boarding houses in the village. He was going to write an editorial about it in *The Record*, but I guess he never did."

"Spring's always going to 'touch things up editorially,'" laughed Harry, "but he generally changes his mind. He's got such a busy mind, Spring has!"

"Well, anyhow, I guess what he said was about so. And I'll bet there aren't half a dozen rooms in town for rent now; and what there are are pretty bum."

"Well, why didn't Phin rent his, then?"

"I don't know. Maybe because the fellows didn't know about it. Last year the house was closed up, you know. Besides, lots and lots of fellows rent their rooms in the spring for the next year."

"All right. Then you think that Sanger will have to take Mrs. Freer's room because it will be the only decent one left, eh?"

"Yes."

"Then where do you come in? And what have I got to do?"

"We've got to make sure that it is the best one left."

"You'll have to talk in words of one syllable," sighed Harry hopelessly, "and illustrate copiously with diagrams. Tell me frankly what the dickens it is you propose to do. Anything short of highway robbery that doesn't require a larger capital than two dollars, you may count me in on."

"Thanks. I propose to see that when Sanger starts to find a new room he won't be able to find anything nearly as good as Mrs. Freer's for any such price. I propose to find out to-morrow just what rooms are for rent. Then I'll see Sanger—and you'll go with me—and we'll tell him about Mrs. Freer's place and get him to look at the room. If he takes it, why, that's all right. If he doesn't, we'll go and get options on the decent rooms, so that when he tries to rent them he won't be able to."

Harry whistled long and expressively. Then he burst into a laugh.

"I thought I was a pretty nifty schemer, Hansel," he said, "but you've got me beaten a city block. Do you think, though, that the boarding-house folks will give us options, as you call it, on their rooms?"

"Yes, because they don't expect to rent them now after school has commenced. They'll be glad to give us refusals of any old rooms they have left. And it won't be necessary to ask many, I guess, because there can't be many rooms for rent at two or three dollars that Sanger would take."

"Well, it sounds all right the way you tell it," said Harry, "but maybe it won't work out just according to specifications. But we'll try it. I'd like mighty well to see Phin and his mother comfortable. If Phin doesn't make his scholarship in January, I guess he will be up against it for fair."

"Yes, but I think he will make it all right. They're letting him make up what he missed while he was out, you know. Now, how can we get hold of Sanger to-morrow?"

"Why to-morrow?" asked Harry. "Let's go and see him this evening and take him to see the room."

"Have you got time?" asked Hansel doubtfully.

"Time? I have more time than money! I'll come over for you at eight, and we'll beard Johnny in his den. By the way, have you spoken to Bert about this?"

"No," answered Hansel.

"Well, I would. He knows Johnny Sanger better than I do. You tell him about it, and get him to go along with us this evening. The more the merrier. And if we can't reason with the silly dub, we'll intimidate him by a show of force."

"All right," laughed Hansel. "I'll look for you at eight."

"Or thereabouts. The fact is, there's a little matter of some fourteen pages of Latin that I think I'll just glance over after supper."

"To hear you talk," said Hansel with a smile, "a fellow would think that you never did a bit of studying! And you always have your lessons better than anyone else, Bert says. You're a fraud!"

Harry grinned as he opened his door with a flourish and ushered the visitor out.

"Not so loud!" he whispered. "It's a secret, and I don't want it known. I'm simply wearing my brain out with study, and I'm afraid that if the faculty hear of it they'll make me stop! Eight o'clock, my boy, or words to that effect. Let us say between eight."

"Between eight and what?" asked Hansel.

"No, just between eight," replied Harry politely, as he closed the door.

Bert was in an extremely contented frame of mind that evening after supper, the result of an article in the paper which predicted defeat for the Fairview football eleven when it met Beechcroft. He read the article to Hansel, and the latter pretended to feel greatly encouraged, although as a matter of fact he placed very little reliance on the writer's powers of prophecy. As soon as he could switch Bert away from the subject of football, which was about the only thing that his roommate thought about in those days, he told about the plan to rent Mrs. Freer's vacant room to Sanger and Shill. The idea appealed to Bert at once.

"Say, that's a scheme, isn't it?" he exclaimed admiringly. "And won't Johnny be mad when we tell him about it afterwards!"

"Well, I hadn't thought of telling him," laughed the other. "Maybe we'd better keep the joke to ourselves."

"Oh, he won't mind after he's got settled at Phin's," said Bert carelessly.

"Just the same, I guess we'll keep it to ourselves," Hansel insisted. "What we want to know is whether you'll go and see Sanger with us this evening. Will you?"

"Oh, but I've got to study!" said Bert blankly.

"But it won't take more than an hour."

"An hour! Thunder! Why, I've got a whole bunch of work to do; and Latin's the hardest ever!"

"Well, have a go at it now. Harry won't be here for three-quarters of an hour."

"Can't," replied Bert. "I've got a couple of plays I want to work out. I've got to do those first. I'll go with you to-morrow night, though."

"You'll go with us to-night," answered Hansel firmly. He switched away the paper from under Bert's pencil and substituted his Latin book. "There! Now find your place and get busy. Here's your dictionary."

Bert looked puzzled, and for a moment seemed half inclined to resent being dictated to. But he evidently thought better of it, for after a moment he laughed, looked regretfully at his diagrams, and bent over the book with a sigh.

"All right," he said. "But I won't go along unless I've got this plaguey stuff by the time Harry comes."

"Oh, you'll have it by then," answered Hansel, as he found his own books and seated himself at the opposite side of the table. "A fellow can learn a lot when he's in the mood for it."

"Humph!" muttered Bert.

At a quarter past eight Harry beat on the door, Hansel shouted "Come in!" and Bert looked up surprisedly from his labor.

"Hello, Harry," he said. "You're just in time. Tell me what this beastly Latin means, will you?"

"When we get back," answered Harry. "You're coming with us to Johnny Sanger's, aren't you?"

Bert stretched his arms above his head and looked undecided.

"I don't know," he said. Then his eyes fell on the diagrams beside him. "Say, I started on those plays before supper and one's about done. Look here, Harry. How's this for a ripping fake? Close formation; see? Ball goes to left half and quarter——"

"Great!" said Harry. "You can tell me about it when we get back. Find his cap, Hansel. He's in a hurry."

Bert got up good-naturedly and laid the diagrams between the pages of his book to mark the place.

"You fellows make me tired," he said. "When I want to study, you won't let me. Why the mischief don't you let Phin rent his own room?"

"Phin's too busy," answered Hansel. "He's in a hole, anyhow, with a week's work to make up. Besides, this is going to be a sort of a surprise."

"Who for?" laughed Bert. "Johnny Sanger?"

"No," said Harry, "for the landladies whose rooms we get the refusals of!"

"It's a bit hard on them, isn't it?" asked Bert virtuously, as he took his cap which Hansel tossed him. "They'll think you mean to take their old rooms."

"Merely a bit of innocent deception," responded Harry airily. "They won't be any worse off than they were before."

"Besides," said Hansel, "if you'll persuade this Sanger chap to rent Mrs. Freer's room we won't have to play tricks on the landladies. And then your conscience won't trouble you, Bert."

"All right; come along. I was cut out for a room-renting agency, anyhow. Besides, Sanger is an awful duffer, anyway, and ought to have worse than this happen to him."

"Worse than this!" exclaimed Harry. "You'd think we were going to haze him to hear you talk! Instead of that we're doing him a real kindness; finding him a nice comfortable room and charging nothing for our services!"

"Guess we'd be doing a heap better," muttered Bert as they went downstairs, "if we minded our own business!"

There was a half moon in the sky and it was very easy to follow the path across the terrace and the green. They made good time and were soon in the village. When they reached the building they sought, they found all its windows dark.

"That's funny," said Hansel, peering up. "Where do you suppose they are?"

"Visiting," answered Bert. "Come on; I'm going back. I've got work to do. The next time I start out on a wild-goose chase with you fellows——"

"Hold on!" said Harry. "There's a light up there, I think. They've got a heavy curtain at the window. Let's go up, anyhow, and make sure."

So they climbed the two flights of narrow stairs, dimly illumined by a bracket lamp on the first landing, and found that Harry was right. Above the door of the room at the front of the building the transom was a dim yellow oblong. Bert knocked and a voice bade them enter.

CHAPTER XIII
FAIRVIEW SENDS A PROTEST

There were two occupants of the room. One, presently identified as Johnny Sanger, was seated in an easy chair, a book in his lap and his slippered feet on the edge of the study table. He was a rather large youth of sixteen years, with a somewhat flat face, prominent brown eyes, a large mouth, and hair of a coppery brown. At the other side of the table sat Shill, tall, narrow, dark-complexioned, and black-haired. Both boys looked surprised when they saw who their visitors were, and as Sanger dropped his feet to the floor and got out of his chair, his expression did not suggest overwhelming delight. Introductions were quickly effected, and the three visitors found seats.

The room, which was poorly lighted by a student's lamp, was larger than appeared from outside, and although the ceiling sloped down on either side to within four feet of the floor, there was a good deal of room there. Two cot beds occupied one end of the room, a washstand was tucked under a dormer window, there was a study table, several chairs, two trunks and a bookcase, and although everything looked very cheap, there was an air of hominess about the place that the visitors found pleasant.

"I hear you fellows have got to move," said Bert presently.

"Yes, hang it all!" answered Sanger. "Just when you find a nice place something goes and happens!"

"When do you go?" Harry inquired politely.

"Last of next week," said Sanger. His roommate was not communicative, but contented himself with observing the callers through his glasses with evident curiosity.

"Found a place yet?" Bert asked.

"Haven't looked. Haven't had time. Mrs. Wagner—she's the woman we rent this of—wants us to go with her. She's taken some sort of a house across the railroad. But that would be too far to walk. Besides, she doesn't half look after things. She's away all day working in the laundry. Say, you'd throw a fit if you looked under the beds and saw the dust there. She makes me tired. Whenever we kick she says she hasn't time, and begins a long song-and-dance about being a poor widow. Hang it, I like things clean, I do!"

"So do I," said Harry cordially. "And look here, if you want a good room where things will be kept spick and span all the time, I can tell you where to look for it."

"Where's that?"

"Mrs. Freer's; know where that is?"

"Yes, that's where Phin Dorr lives. Evan here says she's his mother. Is she?"

"Yes; she was married again after Phin's father died. Well, she's got a room on the first floor that's a peach. Clean? Thunder! You can't find a speck of dust anywhere. It would be just the place for you fellows if you've got to get out of here. And besides that, you'd be doing a real kindness to Phin. You know they haven't any money except what they both make, and I guess it would mean a lot to them to rent this room of theirs."

"Well, we haven't looked around any yet," said Sanger cautiously, with a glance toward his roommate. "We'll have a look at the room, though, to-morrow, and see how we like it. What's the rent, do you know?"

"Three dollars a week," said Hansel.

Sanger shook his head gravely.

"Too much. Everyone's putting their prices down now, you know. It's pretty hard to rent after school begins. I can get all kinds of rooms for two and a half. Why, we only pay about two and a quarter for this!"

"Cheap enough," said Bert. "But then it's a dickens of a long way up here, isn't it?"

"Oh, you get used to it," answered Sanger. "Besides, it's handy for your meals. If we went to Mrs. Freer's I suppose we'd have to walk about three blocks to get anything to eat."

"I think she'd take you to board if you wanted her to," said Hansel.

"How much?"

"I don't know, but I guess she'd do it as cheap as anyone, and she's a mighty good cook too. I know that because I've eaten there."

"Maybe she'd rent for less now that it's so late?" suggested Sanger.

"I don't believe so," replied Harry carelessly. "You see, there aren't many rooms vacant around town now. And, anyhow, this room of hers is worth three."

"Maybe, but we couldn't pay that much, could we, Evan?"

"We wouldn't care to," said Shill cautiously.

"Maybe if you saw the room you would, though," Hansel volunteered. "You wouldn't want to drop around there this evening, I suppose, and look at it? We could go along with you and introduce you."

"Say, how much are you fellows getting for renting it?" asked Sanger with a grin. Bert colored and looked insulted, but Harry interposed with a chuckle.

"I don't blame you for asking that," he answered. "It does look as though we were working on a commission, doesn't it? The fact is, Johnny, we're all fond of Phin, and you know he's had a hard time this fall. So we thought that if we could help him to rent that room we'd do it. Dana heard that you fellows would have to move out in a few days, and it occurred to him that maybe he could help you and Phin at the same time. When he asked me I told him right away that I knew you'd be glad to stretch a point to help Phin."

"Hm!" grunted Sanger dubiously. "That's all well enough, Harry, but if Mrs. What's-her-name wants to rent that room of hers she ought to put the rent down to two and a half at most. If we don't take it, it isn't likely that she'll rent it all the year."

"Oh, you can't tell," answered Harry. "People come and go here. She's not worrying about that. Supposing, though, we all walk down there together, and we'll ask what her best price is."

"Oh, I guess we don't care to go to-night," said Sanger. "It's late and I've got my slippers on. Evan and I'll look at the place in the morning on the way up to school. Of course I'd be glad to do anything I could to help Phin, but three dollars is a whole lot to pay for a room at this time of the year, and I don't believe I could afford it."

"Well, we thought we'd mention it to you," said Harry, arising. "No harm done, eh? We wanted you to have a chance at it, but if you think it's too high, all right. You might ask Mrs. Freer if she'll take less, you know; maybe she will. But I know very well that I wouldn't if I were she. She's got one of the best rooms in town, and ought to get a fair price. Hope you fellows will find what you want; but there aren't many rooms for rent now, they say, so you needn't be disappointed if you don't find anything right away. I guess we'll be going on."

Once more on the street Hansel turned to Harry.

"What do you think?" he asked eagerly.

"Oh, he'd take the room in a minute if she'd offer it to him for two and a half. He will go around there in the morning and try to beat her down. And I'm afraid he will do it, too."

"Well, maybe she'd be glad to get it off her hands for two and a half," said Bert.

"Maybe she would," Harry answered. "But Sanger can pay three and I'm going to see that he does it."

"How?" asked Hansel.

"I'm going to stop there now, see Phin and tell him to make his mother promise not to come down on her price."

"What are you going to tell Phin?"

"No more than I have to. I'll tell him that Sanger and Shill are looking for a room, that they can pay three, and will do it if they have to. Then to-morrow you and I, Hansel, will hike around and get a refusal on every decent room there is left."

"That's great!" said Bert. "I'd go around with you and help, only I'm afraid I'd get sort of mixed up and hire the rooms by mistake. Landladies can do anything they want with me. The first year I was here I couldn't get on the campus, and I went to look at a room at Mrs. Stevens's place. It was a beast of a room, but she took me up three flights of stairs and went to a lot of trouble to show it and so—well, first thing I knew I had taken it for the year!"

"You'd better keep out of it, I guess," laughed Hansel. "And supposing Bert and I go on to the corner and wait for you, Harry? If we all go in Phin may suspect something. You know he'd forbid us to do what we're doing if he found out about it."

"Don't see why," Bert objected.

"He would, though," said Hansel stoutly. "We'll wait for you at the corner. Don't stay long; it's getting frosty."

Harry was back in ten minutes or so, reporting that Phin had agreed to keep the price up, and the three conspirators walked briskly back to school.

The next morning Hansel and Harry were extremely busy, so busy that each was obliged to absent himself from one recitation, a thing much easier to do than to explain subsequently. By dinner time they had canvassed the town of Bevan Hills very thoroughly, and had between them discovered just five rooms which might possibly answer the requirements of Messrs. Sanger and Shill. And in each case they had secured the refusal of the apartment. The landladies had given up hope of renting the empty rooms that year, and when Hansel or Harry professed to be unable to reach a decision, and asked that they be given an option for a few days, their request was readily granted, especially as they in no case expressed dissatisfaction with the price quoted.

"I guess now," said Harry, "it's up to Sanger to either go across the railroad with his Dutch lady or take Phin's room."

Had Sanger been suspiciously inclined the solicitude displayed by Harry and Hansel and Bert during the next few days might have suggested more to him than it did.

"Found a room yet?" they asked him regularly every morning and afternoon, and Sanger would shake his head and acknowledge that he hadn't. At first he was rather superior about it, seeking to convey the idea that he had a good many apartments in view, and was only undecided which was more worthy of the honor of sheltering him, but on the third day there was a worried, perplexed tone in his voice.

"No," he said, "I haven't found a room yet, and I don't believe I'm going to. The landladies are crazy, I guess; asking me three and even three and a half at this time of year! And there are only three or four decent rooms in town, anyway."

"Well, you only want one," said Bert cheerfully.

"Yes, but I can't get the promise of even one! Everywhere I go they tell me that some one has the refusal of the room just now, but if I'll leave my name they'll let me know in a few days. Why, we've got to get out of our present quarters by Friday!"

"Too bad you couldn't have taken that room at Mrs. Freer's," said Hansel. "That would have been a pretty good place for you fellows."

"Well, we may take it yet," answered Sanger, "if the old lady'll come down a bit on her price."

"Oh, then it isn't rented?" asked Hansel in simulated surprise.

"It wasn't yesterday," answered Sanger. "Did you hear that it was taken?"

"N-no, only I know that there was some one looking at that room two nights ago, and I heard that they liked it first rate. But maybe they haven't actually taken it yet. Too bad, though, for that was certainly a dandy room. Well, I hope you find something, Sanger."

"Maybe you'll decide to go with your present landlady," suggested Bert. "It isn't bad across the railroad, they say. I never knew any fellow that lived there, but I've heard that if you didn't mind kids it wasn't so bad. Of course, it'll be a pretty fierce walk in winter!"

"Oh, I'm not going there," muttered Sanger. "That's out of the question. I'll find a place to-day or to-morrow, all right. If you see Phin Dorr, Dana, I wish you'd find out about that room for me. And if it isn't rented you might tell him that I'm thinking about it, and will pay two dollars and seventy-five cents. It's worth that, don't you think, Bert?"

"Sure! It's worth what they ask, I think."

"Not at this time of year," said Sanger doggedly.

"I don't see that the time of year has got much to do with it," said Hansel a trifle impatiently. "You say yourself that there are only three or four rooms vacant that you'd have and that you can't get even those. Seems to me the supply and demand are only about equal. Considering the scarcity of good rooms I don't see why the landladies don't put their prices up instead of reducing them!"

"But who do you suppose are after rooms now?" asked Sanger. "Awfully funny, I call it. I'll bet the women just tell me that to make me pay their prices. I don't believe they've given refusals to folks!"

"But even if they haven't," said Hansel, "their prices are too high, aren't they?"

"Yes," growled Sanger. "They're all trying to hold me up, because they know I've got to have a room right away. I've got a good mind to fool them and——"

"Live across the railroad?" asked Bert.

"No," answered the other defiantly, "take that room at Phin's place!"

"Well, I wouldn't decide right away," said Hansel soothingly. "Besides, I dare say you're too late for Phin's room."

"I wish I knew," said Sanger troubledly.

"What does Shill think about it?" Bert asked.

"Oh, he likes that room the best, but he will go wherever I say," said Sanger carelessly. "I guess—I guess I'll see if I can find Phin. Mrs. Freer said she'd board us for three and a half apiece, and if she'd only knock off a quarter on her room, I'd take it in a minute. And I think she would if it wasn't for Phin. He's making her hold out on me. I should think that he'd be glad to rent at a decent price if he's so hard up."

"Maybe he's had a better offer," Bert suggested.

Sanger moved away, looking anxious.

"We've got him hooked all right enough," said Bert. "But, say, what was that yarn you were telling about some one looking at the room and liking it?"

"Oh, that was Harry, the night before last. He told me that he got Phin to show him the room, and that he thought it was cheap at three dollars."

"Oh!" laughed Bert. "Well, you certainly got Johnny worried! I'll bet he engages that room before night."

But he didn't. Having learned from Phin that it was still for rent, he stuck out for the twenty-five cent reduction. Phin would gladly have rented at that price, if only to be rid of Sanger's importunities, but he had solemnly promised Harry that he'd hold out for the full price of three dollars a week, and meant to keep that promise. It was hard work, though, for Phin wanted very much to rent the room, and every time Sanger left him he feared that he wouldn't come back. He sought Harry that evening and laid the matter before him.

"Of course," said Phin, "I'd be glad to get that extra quarter, but I'd hate to lose the chance of renting the room, Harry. And I'm afraid now that Sanger will go somewhere else. Don't you think I'd better tell him he can have it for two seventy-five?"

Harry hesitated, wondering whether a compromise wasn't advisable. Finally:

"I tell you, Phin," he said. "I'm going to hold you to your agreement until three o'clock to-morrow. After that you can let him have it for any price you like. How does that suit you?"

"Well, I suppose I've got to be satisfied," said Phin with a smile. "Whose room is this, anyway, Harry?"

"It's yours, old son, but you're not able to rent it to the best advantage. That's where I come in. I'm legal counsel, don't you see? Hold on until three to-morrow, Phin, and I'll guarantee that he will come around to your figure. Remember that it isn't the twenty-five cents we're fighting for, but the principle of the thing!"

"Oh," said Phin, "is that it? And—er—what is the principle?"

"The principle?" Harry threw one knee over the other, joined the tips of his fingers, and looked over the tops of a pair of imaginary spectacles. "The principle involved in this case, Mr. Dorr, is—ah—er—well, in short, Phin,

Johnny Sanger has as much money as any fellow in school, and it isn't right for him to be so close with it. The habit will grow on him and he'll become a miser. It behooves his friends to combat this tendency and—and—there you are, Phin! Simple, isn't it?"

After Phin had gone, Harry went over to see Hansel and Bert, and the three held a council of war. It was agreed that it would be advisable for Harry and Hansel to make a trip into town in the morning and strengthen their defenses. And this was done. The landladies were not so compliant to-day, for Sanger had been around looking at their rooms. But in each case either Hansel or Harry managed to secure a promise that the room would not be rented until the following afternoon. And as the following day was Friday, they thought that the promise was liberal enough. They hurried back to school for a ten o'clock recitation, and awaited events. At two o'clock the battle was won. Sanger informed Hansel of the fact, only he didn't put it exactly that way.

"I've taken that room at Mrs. Freer's," he said, "and we're going to move in to-morrow afternoon."

"That's good," answered Hansel, concealing his satisfaction. "How much are you going to pay? I suppose she knocked off that quarter?"

Sanger's face darkened.

"No, she didn't," he said. "But I thought there wasn't any use in making a fuss about twenty-five cents. I hate anything small."

"Well, I'm glad you've got it," answered Hansel, trying his best not to smile. "I think you'll like it."

"Thanks. Come and see us some time."

Hansel nodded and waved as Sanger hurried on.

That afternoon Hansel and Harry got together and wrote notes regretfully informing the landladies that their rooms would not be required. And the next afternoon, Sanger, surrounded by his goods and chattels, sat in the first-floor room at Mrs. Freer's, and perplexedly perused four notes, which in each case informed him that he could now engage the room he had looked at, since the party who had the refusal had decided not to rent.

"Well, that's a funny thing!" exclaimed Sanger.

But he never learned the truth of the matter. Nor, for that matter, did Phin. The conspirators relieved their consciences by declaring that the deception had been practiced in a good cause, but they weren't particular about having the facts known.

Life in 22 Prince was much pleasanter those days. Bert's gratitude to Hansel, awkwardly displayed though it was, seemed to the younger boy almost pathetic. There were long talks in the evening on the football situation, and Hansel's opinions were solicited and deferred to in a way that was almost embarrassing. The subject of Cameron's standing was not discussed; Hansel realized the futility of trying to make Bert look at the question from his point of view; and at length he even found himself sympathizing with the other's attitude; the consuming passion of Bert's life at that time was to bring his captaincy to a successful termination with a victory over Fairview, and if he was willing to stretch fairness a little to do it, he was not without the support of precedent. During those two weeks preceding the final combat of the football campaign Bert and Hansel got to know and understand each other, and a mutual liking, which all the autumn had been only awaiting an opportunity, sprang up and ripened ultimately into a firm friendship.

On Wednesday, after practice was over, Hansel heard his name called as he was trotting across the green toward the terrace and Weeks Hall. He turned and found Billy Cameron overtaking him. Not without some embarrassment he waited for the other to catch up.

"Hello, Cameron," he said.

"Hello," responded the other as he ranged himself alongside. "Say, Dana, I wish you'd tell me something."

"All right, I will if I can."

"Well, it's this: have you got anything against me?"

"Not a thing—personally," answered Hansel.

"Well, why can't you and those other beggars let me alone?" asked Cameron. "I've never interfered with you chaps."

"I don't think there's one of us who doesn't like you, Cameron," answered Hansel after a moment. "And if we're down on you it isn't for what you are, but for what you represent."

"Represent?" repeated Billy with a puzzled laugh. "Gee! I didn't know I represented anything. What is it?"

"'Gee! I didn't know I represented anything!'"

"What I mean is this: we haven't any right to play a fellow on our football team or our baseball team who is here just for football or baseball, who is having his way through school paid by the fellows. If we once countenance that sort of thing, Cameron, it's going to lead us a long way off the right track. If it's fair in your case, why not in other cases? What's to keep us from hiring a whole team of good football players?"

"Couldn't afford it," answered Billy practically.

"Not this year, but there's no telling what might be done in that way. For my part, I'm sorry I've had to—to worry you, but unfortunately, Cameron, you've placed yourself in a wrong position."

"Now, look here," said the other mildly. "You say I'm here just to play football. That isn't so, Dana. I may not be very smart at lessons, and my folks haven't any money, but I'm not a mucker. I got fired out of the other school because I couldn't keep up, but why couldn't I? Because the fellows I knew didn't study, and because the faculty was down on me from the start. Then some fellows here wrote and asked me to come here; said I wouldn't have to worry about expenses. Well, I came. I wanted to get ready for college somehow, and this seemed a good chance. They gave me a place in dining hall that supplied my meals, and they paid my tuition. What's the difference whether they paid it or some one else? I know two or three fellows here who are having their tuition paid by friends, and not by their own folks. But they don't play football, and so there's no kick. Last year, if I didn't get honors, I was pretty well up in my class, and this year I'm trying for a scholarship. If I get it, and Farrel says I'll stand a good show, the fellows can keep their old money; I'd a heap rather pay my own way, you bet!"

"But—but some one's coaching you, aren't they?"

"Who, me? No, sir, I haven't had an hour's coaching since I came here. Mr. Farrel's been mighty good to me, and he's helped me a lot with Latin, but I haven't had any coaching."

"Oh, I understood you had," answered Hansel.

"Well, I haven't. It's been mighty tough work sometimes, but now it isn't so hard. I've learned more here last year and this than I did all the four years I was at Bursley. As for football, I like to play it, but if the fellows are going to make a fuss about it, I guess I can get along without it."

"If you could only get along without the money from the football fund," said Hansel eagerly, "you could play all you wanted to and no one would say a word."

"Well, if I can get a hundred-dollar scholarship I'll pay for myself, you bet! Of course, if I don't get it, and the fellows don't want to pay the rest of my tuition, I'll just have to leave. But I don't want to, Dana; I like this old school; the fellows are decent to me, and so are the instructors; they don't make me feel that I'm no good because I haven't any money, like they did at Bursley. Mind, I don't hold it against you fellows for what you're doing. Maybe you've got the right end of it. I don't pretend to understand it; at Bursley we got fellows wherever we could find 'em, and we paid them to play for us. Maybe it ain't right; I don't know. But I don't want any fellow to say I haven't earned what they've given me here; I may not be so—so particular as you chaps, but I never cheated anyone out of a cent or took a cent I hadn't earned."

"I'm sorry," answered Hansel. "I suppose I started the row, and I think the way we look at the matter is the right one, but it seems hard on you, Cameron. All I hope is, you'll get your scholarship, pay your own way and stay here to play for us another year."

"That's fair talk," said the other heartily. "I was afraid you had it in for me—er—personally, as you say. And I didn't like that because—well, you play a fine game of football and—and seem white; I like white fellows like you and Bert and Harry and Larry Royle. This where you live? Well, I'm glad I had a talk with you. Whenever you hear any fellow say that Billy Cameron isn't playing fair you tell me about it, will you?"

"Yes," answered Hansel gravely. "Good night. Come up and see us some time."

"All right, I'll try to. But I'm pretty busy just now; that Ovid chap has me lashed to the mast. Do you have him?"

"I had him last year."

"Tough, ain't he? Good night."

"Good night," echoed Hansel with a smile.

He thought of Billy Cameron a good deal that evening, and when, next day, a shell from the enemy's lines at Fairview fell unexpectedly into camp and plunged the Beechcroft hosts into confusion and consternation, he remembered him again and, in spite of a natural feeling of exultation at the successful outcome of his efforts, was genuinely sorry for him.

The shell hurled by the enemy was a protest against the playing of William Cameron, who, the Fairview authorities declared, was not eligible, if their information was correct, to play on the Beechcroft team. By noon the news was all over school, and had become the all-absorbing subject of discussion and conjecture. Bert was for playing Cameron whether Fairview liked it or not, but Mr. Ames vetoed that plan.

"The matter will be placed before Dr. Lambert," he stated to Bert and Harry, who had sought him for consultation. "He will have to decide. If he says Cameron may play, it will be all right; Fairview will have to put up with him. If he doesn't, you'll have to get along without him."

"He'll say no," answered Bert bitterly.

"Maybe. I'll see him this evening."

"What I'd like to know," exclaimed Harry with annoyance, "is how they found it out! Some one must have told them."

Mr. Ames was gravely silent.

CHAPTER XIV
THE SPIRIT OF THE SCHOOL

When at nine o'clock that evening Mr. Ames returned from his conference with the principal, he found his study occupied by Bert, Harry, Cameron, and Cotton, who for the better part of an hour had impatiently awaited his return and the doctor's decision in regard to the playing of the right half back. Mr. Ames's report was disappointing to Harry, who had hoped for an affirmative decision, and agreeable to Bert, who had feared the worst. The doctor, explained Mr. Ames, would leave the decision to the school. A meeting would be called for to-morrow evening, the case would be put before the fellows by Mr. Ames and a majority vote would decide the matter.

"Good!" cried Bert. "We'll win!"

He spent the next day, as did other members of the team, in securing support for his side. Cameron himself, however, took no part in the proceedings; in fact, to see him one would have thought him the last person in school to be interested by what was going on.

At half-past seven, the hour set for the meeting, the hall was filled to the doors. Even the "towners," who as a rule were not to be dragged back to the academy after supper, were present in force. In fact, it is safe to say that every student physically able to reach Academy Hall was on hand when Mr. Ames called the meeting to order.

Just as quiet prevailed, a newcomer arrived, and made his way up the center aisle to the platform. There was a long moment of breathless surprise; then the clapping began and grew to a veritable tempest of applause. Never before since his connection with Beechcroft had Dr. Lambert attended a meeting of the students, save at commencement time, and the fellows were at once surprised and flattered. The doctor, too, seemed a bit surprised, probably at the length and vigor of the applause, but whether he felt flattered I cannot say. Mr. Ames lifted a chair to the platform for him and he subsided into it gravely, folded his arms and looked slowly about the room. With the doctor's advent the meeting seemed to take on a more serious aspect, the question to be decided suddenly assumed a larger importance, and the fellows presented an attentiveness so respectful and silent as to appear almost alarming.

Mr. Ames presented the case briefly and fairly, and ended by stating that the decision rested with the fellows. "If," he concluded, "you honestly believe that Cameron should be permitted to represent the academy a week from to-morrow, you will vote so. On the other hand, if you honestly think that he should not be permitted to play, you will vote so. The sentiment of the majority will be accepted by Dr. Lambert as the sentiment of the school, and will be accepted as final. We will have a standing vote, if you please."

"One moment, please." Dr. Lambert held up his hand toward the instructor and arose from his chair. There was a slight clapping of hands which died out as the principal walked to the front of the platform.

"I wish to say," began the doctor, "that your decision this evening will decide a question of more importance than whether Mr. Cameron is to play football for you, which, while it probably seems to you to be of great moment, is of really little consequence. I understand that without the services of Mr. Cameron, you may be beaten in your game of football, but that would not be a very grave calamity. I believe this school has been beaten before, and we are alive to tell the tale. I hope you will win. I know very little about the game, but I intend to be on hand a week from to-morrow, if my duties will allow, and learn something about it; and, naturally, I should prefer to witness a victory rather than a defeat.

"But there are two ways of securing victory. One way is by fair means, honestly, aboveboard; the other way is by unfair methods, by questionable tricks, by deceitful subterfuge. As far as I am concerned personally, I should prefer to witness an honorable defeat rather than a victory won by underhand methods. I hope you all would. Note, if you please, that I am not inferring that you have any intention of sacrificing honor to the lust of winning. I make no such charge. I know so little of athletics, that I do not pretend to be able to judge infallibly the intricate points involved. I am leaving such judgment to you. And whatever your decision may be, I shall accept it.

"Mr. Ames has spoken to you this evening of what he calls school spirit. What I understand by school spirit is the moral attitude taken by the school as a body in regard to the problems, large and small, which daily present themselves in school life. School spirit is an important factor, I might almost say the most important factor, of an institution of learning. Handsome buildings, a capable teaching corps, liberal endowments, beautiful surroundings, all these may fail to create a good school so long as the school spirit is wrong. A faculty may lay down laws and enforce them, prescribe rules of conduct for study hours and recreation hours, watch, guide, and instruct, and yet fail miserably in the creation of a perfect school. Those laws and rules, that guidance and instruction, must have the spirit of the school back of them, or else they are worth no more than the paper they are inscribed upon. The student is the school; if he cares less for the benefits to be attained by faithful attention to his studies than he does to the pleasure and fleeting distinction to be won in athletics, the school will not thrive for any length of time; if he holds the end to be of more importance than the means, either in the schoolroom or on the athletic field, the school will never attain to a position of honor among institutions of its kind.

"School spirit is the foundation, then. And school spirit is of the students, not of the faculty. The faculty may influence it, it cannot form it. It is so intangible that the cleverest faculty cannot lay its hand upon it and say, 'Here it is; I will mold it to suit me.' It is a tree toward which the faculty plays the part of gardener. Its growth is its own. The gardener may aid it or stunt it; he may, with infinite pains, extending over a long period, direct the growth of the branches, but that is as much as he can do; for when all is said, he is only the gardener, and the tree is Nature.

"The spirit of the school is as vital here as elsewhere. And when I said a few moments ago that your decision this evening would decide a matter of more consequence than the fate of Mr. Cameron in regard to the football game, I meant that you would determine how the spirit of your school stands with regard to athletics. If you say to-night that it stands in favor of virtually hiring athletes to win your games for you—mind, I do not say whether this is right or wrong; you are to decide that for yourselves—then you have committed it to a sentiment which is likely to influence it for some time. In short, you will be, I firmly believe, deciding not alone for this year, but for several years to come. That is all I have to say."

The doctor bowed gravely and took his seat again. There was a slight clatter of applause which speedily died away for want of support. Mr. Ames glanced questioningly at the principal. The latter nodded, and the coach arose again.

"As I put the question, those in favor of the motion will arise and remain standing until counted. Mr. Foote, will you kindly take the left of the aisle?"

The physical director frowned through his glasses in a surprised manner, nodded his head, and stood up uninterestedly.

"Those in favor of allowing Mr. Cameron to play will rise," directed Mr. Ames.

There was a shuffling of feet, and here and there throughout the meeting fellows arose, some hesitatingly, some briskly, and stood to be counted. On a bench near the front Hansel and Phin were the only ones who remained seated, while beside them Bert, Harry, Royle and other members of the first and second teams were on their feet. Cameron, at the end of the next bench, kept his place, viewing the proceedings with a perplexed frown. After all, he was a modest chap, and all this fuss and turmoil seemed to him very silly. If they didn't want him, why not say so? Bert, glancing over the hall, looked at first bewildered, then angry. Mr. Ames turned questioningly to Mr. Foote.

"Seventeen," said the latter wearily.

"And thirty-five here," said Mr. Ames. "In all fifty-two. Be seated, please. Now those opposed will kindly stand up."

It was unnecessary to count them, but the count was made, nevertheless.

"A total of seventy-eight," announced Mr. Ames. "There appears to be no doubt as to the sense of the meeting." He turned to Dr. Lambert. "Did you wish to say anything more?"

The principal shook his head.

"May I speak, sir?" It was Cameron.

"I believe there's no objection," responded Mr. Ames.

Billy moved out into the aisle and faced the meeting, rather red of face and somewhat embarrassed of manner, but doggedly.

"I just want to say," he began in a low voice that grew louder as he gained confidence, "I just want to say to you fellows that it's all right as far as I'm concerned. I want to do what's right. If you think I oughtn't to play, why, that's enough for me. I want to be fair and square all around. You fellows have paid sixty dollars of my tuition for me, and I'm much obliged to you. But I'd like to have you know that I mean to pay it back to you just as soon as I can, because you expected me to play in the Fairview game, and I'm not going to do it. I don't want to take money and not deliver the goods.

"I don't believe my not playing is going to make all the difference you fellows think. We've got a good team and we ought to lick the—" Billy glanced toward Dr. Lambert—"we ought to beat Fairview without much trouble. If I can't play I can help things along, I suppose, and I'll do it all I know how. And—and I guess that's all. Thank you."

He squeezed his way back to his seat amid a roar of applause that lasted several moments. When it subsided Spring was asking recognition, and Mr. Ames nodded to him.

"Mr. Chairman and—and fellows," began Spring eagerly, "it seems to me that Cameron shouldn't be allowed to pay back that money. He's played all the fall, in every game, and it seems to me he's earned it already. And if he takes hold, as he offers to do, and helps the coaches, he will have more than earned it. I don't believe there's a fellow here to-night who doesn't honor Cameron for a fine, plucky player, and a good, honest fellow. And I think he ought to understand that, in spite of—of circumstances, we're right with him. And I'd like to propose a good big cheer for him!"

And so the meeting ended, incongruously enough, with the spectacle of a fellow who had just been barred out of the football team being cheered to the echo!

For two days Bert was hopeless and glum. But by Monday he began to cheer up again. The showing of the team, composed as it had been almost entirely of second string players, in the game with Parksboro had been highly satisfactory, and this, combined with the fact that Billy Cameron was coaching the half backs, and Lockhard, who was slated for his position, in particular, with evident success, brought encouragement to Bert. Besides Cameron several graduates put in an appearance Monday and Tuesday and assisted with the coaching. Interest and excitement grew with each passing day until on Friday night, what with the mass meeting and the old boys who were sprinkled through the dormitories, sleep in any respectable amount came to the eyes of but few.

Saturday dawned bright and crisp, an ideal day for the middle of November. The trees were bare of limb, and the beech leaves which for long had lain huddled in drifts along the walks and roads, had lost their pale golden hue. But the sky was fair, the sun shone brightly, and in warm nooks and corners the grass yet held its color.

From the station to the academy, almost every house and store proved its loyalty by the display of light blue. Before the little white house across from the Congregational church, behind whose sitting-room window Mrs. Freer, quite recovered from her illness, sat and sewed and watched the passing with smiling eyes behind their spectacles, a Beechcroft banner had fluttered valiantly since early dawn, placed there by Phin ere he had started on his morning round of the furnaces in his charge.

At ten Phin showed up at 22 Prince, a knot of pale blue ribbon in his lapel. He found Bert and Hansel in and for a while the three sat and won the game and lost it, and won it again many times. Then Harry demanded admittance, and strode in bearing, what at first looked like a flag of truce, but which on second sight proved to be a white sweater.

"There you are," he cried, tossing the garment at Hansel. "There's your old ill-gotten gains. Hope it gets you into as much trouble as it has me!"

"I'd forgotten all about it," said Hansel truthfully. "And I'm not going to take it."

"Suit yourself," answered Harry with a shrug. "I'm through with it."

"What it is and all about it?" demanded Bert. Harry explained the one-sided wager whereby Hansel was to come into possession of the white sweater if Cameron didn't play in to-day's game.

"But I don't intend to take it," said Hansel earnestly. "It doesn't seem right; seems as though I was profiting by Cameron's misfortune."

"Don't worry about Billy," said Harry. "He's as chipper as a lark; says if Lockhard plays the game the way he's taught him to, he won't mind not playing himself!"

"I tell you what, Harry!" exclaimed Hansel.

"All right; what?"

"Why, you won't keep it and I won't take it, so give it to Cameron."

"Billy?"

"Why not? I'll bet he hasn't got a good sweater to his name."

"Brilliant youth!" cried Harry, bolting for the door. "I'll do it!"

Lunch was served to the team at half-past eleven, and at half-past twelve they were sent to stroll around the grounds. The game was to begin at two, but long before that hour the stands were filled, and the ropes behind the side lines were sagging under the pressure of the spectators unable to secure seats. The light blue of Beechcroft and the red and blue of Fairview were everywhere in evidence, and waved and fluttered when, at a few minutes before two, the teams trotted on.

There was ten minutes of practice, the rival captains met in the center of the field and watched a coin spin upward and down in the sunlight, the teams arranged themselves over the faded turf, with its glistening new lines of whitewash, there was a moment of quiet, broken by the shrill pipe of a whistle, and the big game had begun.

CHAPTER XV
THE GAME WITH FAIRVIEW

The first half of the Beechcroft-Fairview game may be easily disposed of. There was no scoring, nor did either team get within scoring distance of the opponent's goal. From the moment Beechcroft kicked off, and the Fairview left tackle caught the ball and brought it back ten yards before being downed, the battle raged hotly in the center of the field. Not once did Fairview get beyond her enemy's thirty-yard line, and not once did Beechcroft penetrate even so far into the opponent's territory. After a few tries at the ends, which ended disastrously for her, Fairview buckled down to hammer-and-tongs football. There were no weak places in the light-blue line, and time and time again Fairview failed by the merest fraction of a foot to gain her distance. There was almost no kicking. On one occasion, having been driven back to her twenty-five yards, Beechcroft punted, in the hope that Fairview would fumble. But, although Hansel was waiting beside the red-and-blue left half back when the ball came down, that player went to earth with the oval firmly clasped.

It was uninteresting playing, or it would have been, had not the two or three thousand persons who looked on been enthusiastic partisans. The worst of it all, from a Beechcroft point of view, was that during that first period of play, Fairview showed herself a little better in defense, and noticeably stronger in attack. When the whistle blew, the two teams, panting and exhausted, were above Beechcroft's thirty-five-yard line. The home team, joined by the blanketed substitutes, trotted up the terrace to the gymnasium, while the visitors retired into the shelter of the two barges which had brought them from the station. The crowd moved about, such as were not fearful of losing good seats, and for ten minutes the green presented a scene of gayety quite unwonted. Then back came the light-blue players, and were welcomed with thundering cheers; and out tumbled the Fairview men and received their meed of applause.

Beechcroft had the west goal. It was Fairview's kick-off. Bert received the ball and made well over twenty yards through a crowded field. An attempt to get around Fairview's left end lost four yards, Conly being thrown back. A tandem play with Bert carrying the ball netted three yards. On third down, with six yards to gain, Cotton kicked. The ball went almost straight into the air and came down into the crowd. Love, the Beechcroft left tackle, recovered it. After that, by alternate attacks at guards and tackles, Beechcroft advanced the ball by a series of short rushes for thirty yards. On the opponent's thirty-eight yards she was held for downs, and the pigskin went to the red and blue.

Fairview began a merciless hammering at the right side of Beechcroft's line, confining her attention largely to Mulford at tackle. Beechcroft's hopes dwindled. Back down the field advanced the red and blue, slowly at first, then, as Mulford weakened, faster and faster, making gains of three, four, even six yards at a time. Hansel went to the rescue of his tackle, and Lockhard and Bert threw themselves time and again at his back. Had the secondary defense not been what it was the story of the second half might be speedily told. On her twenty yards, Beechcroft called for time. Mulford, weak and white, and woe-begone, was taken out and Carew took his place. A tentative try at the newcomer proved to Fairview that she must look elsewhere for consistent gains. A clever double pass enabled her quarter to get around King, at left end, and he reeled off twelve precious yards before Cotton nabbed him. Beechcroft was now almost at her last ditch, and a score for the red and blue looked certain. A tandem went through for two yards between Royle and Stevens, and the Fairview right half dug himself into Love for one more. Then it was third down, with two to go. Beechcroft was almost under her crossbar; only five yards lay between the ball and the goal line. From across the field came the incessant appeals of the light-blue adherents to "*Hold 'em! Hold 'em! Hold 'em!*"

And hold them she did. Not an inch was gained by the next play, although the Fairview tandem smashed viciously at right guard and the balance of the team threw themselves behind it. The attack was crumpled up, and when the piled-up mass of bodies was disentangled the ball lay fairly on the white line.

Down the field sailed the ball, and under it raced Hansel. On Fairview's forty yards it plumped into the arms of the red-and-blue quarter who, the next instant, was on his face on the turf, three yards nearer his goal, with Hansel hugging his legs. Then it began all over again, that remorseless charge down the field. Fairview's fast, heavy backs crashed into the opponent's line for short, steady gains. Near the middle of the field the light blue received the ball on penalty, only to lose it again the next moment by a fumbled pass from Cotton to Lockhard. A weak place suddenly developed at center, where Royle, despite his size and weight, had been clearly outplayed all along by the man opposite him who, although many pounds lighter, was quick and heady. Past Beechcroft's thirty yards crashed the conquerors, past her twenty-five, past her twenty. Then time was called for an injury to Bert. But even as the spectators discussed hopelessly or cheerfully, according to the colors they wore, what would happen if the Beechcroft captain was taken out, he was up again and was limping along his line, thumping the fellows on back or shoulder, and hoarsely calling upon them to hold.

Two downs netted Fairview three yards. Captain and quarter held a consultation, and then right half dropped back for a place kick from the thirty-yard line. Quarter threw himself upon the turf, and the onlookers held their breaths. Back flew the ball on a good pass, quarter caught it, turned it, cocked it toward the crossbar, and right half, with a quick glance toward the goal, stepped forward and kicked. But Beechcroft, goaded by desperation, had broken through, and the ball rebounded from Stevens's broad chest as he sprang into the air. Half a dozen men threw themselves toward it, but it was Royle who captured it.

For a time the tide of fortune seemed to have turned. Beechcroft hammered desperately at the Fairview line and managed to work the ball back to her fifty-yard line. But there Carew was caught holding, and Fairview received fifteen yards. Cotton kicked poorly, and it was Fairview's ball again on her fifty-three yards. Once more the advance began. But this time each attack brought a longer gain. Beechcroft was weakening all along her line. On her forty yards the Fairview quarter, fearful perhaps that not enough time remained in which to cover the remaining distance by line plunging, tried a run and got away without difficulty between Love and King, the latter allowing himself to be put entirely out of the play. But Conly tackled him at the end of ten- or twelve-yard sprint, and the fierce plunges at the center began again. This time, surely, thought the watchers, nothing could stay Fairview's progress. Twice Beechcroft had valiantly staved off defeat, but that she could do so again was too much to expect. Yet as her opponent neared the goal, the light blue's defense strengthened. Past the twenty-five-yard line crept the foe, yet succeeding attacks netted shorter and shorter gains, and over on the stands the Beechcroft supporters took courage and never paused in their cheering. Twelve yards from the goal line the advance stopped. The Fairview left tackle, at the head of a tandem, was hurled back for a loss, and the ball went to Beechcroft.

There remained but four minutes of playing time. On the Beechcroft stand and along the right of the upper side of the field pale-blue flags waved and flourished, and voices hoarsely shouted their delight. Beechcroft's only hope now was to keep her rival from scoring; all idea of winning the game herself had long since passed away; a no-score game would be enough. On the side line Mr. Ames, watching grimly, mentally petitioned the Fates for an 0 to 0 result. But perhaps the Fates didn't hear him.

Cotton, realizing that their only hope lay in keeping the ball out of Fairview's hands for the next four minutes decided not to kick until forced to. On the first play the ball went to Bert, and Bert, aching, wearied, limping, smashed his way like a cyclone through Fairview's line for five yards. Again he was given the ball, but this time no gain resulted. Then it was Lockhard's turn, and he managed to get a bare yard outside of right tackle. With four yards to gain on third down, a kick or a fake was the only hope. Cotton decided upon the latter. He dropped back to the five-yard line, the defense formed about him, and Royle passed back the ball. But it never reached Cotton, in spite of the fact that he went through the motions of catching and kicking it, and in spite of the fact that half the opposing team rushed down upon him. Lockhard had the pigskin nestled into the crook of his elbow, and was streaking around the right end of his line with a small but well-working interference. Hansel had put the opposing tackle out of the way, and Bert had sent the Fairview end sprawling on his back, and through the resulting hole Lockhard had sped. Ten yards beyond, Bert, handicapped by a wrenched knee, dropped back and only Lockhard and Hansel kept up the running.

"Lockhard ... was streaking around the right end of his line."

But now the field, friend and foe alike, had taken up the chase, while ahead, coming warily down upon them, was the Fairview quarter back. Both Lockhard and Hansel were fast runners, though the latter could at any time have outstripped the other. For the moment danger from behind was not pressing, and Hansel gave all his attention to the foe ahead. Running abreast of Lockhard, he called to that youth to keep out. Then he made straight for the quarter back. But the latter was an old hand, and was not to be drawn from his quarry. As they came together, Hansel found with dismay, that the enemy had fooled him, and had got between him and Lockhard. Desperately Hansel crashed into him, but the quarter, giving before the attack, kept his feet, and the next instant sprang at Lockhard.

Down went the latter just as Hansel, swinging about, swerved to the rescue, and as he fell the ball bounded from his grasp and went bobbing erratically toward the side line. Hansel was on it like a cat on a mouse, and before the quarter or the nearest of the pursuit could reach him had dropped upon it, found his feet again after rolling over twice, and was off once more toward Fairview's goal.

From the sides of the field came a confused inarticulate roar as the spectators, on their feet, watched with anxious hearts the outcome of the race. Five yards ahead of the nearest pursuer sped Hansel, running like a flash. Behind him, with outstretched, clutching hands, ran the Fairview right end. Back of him friend and foe were strung along the field. Hansel's feet twinkled above the thirty-yard line. Beside him, dangerously near, was the white boundary line, but he dared not edge farther toward the middle of the gridiron lest it prove his undoing. Another white line streak passed beneath him, and then a second. The goal line was clearly in view. But he had played through almost seventy minutes of a hard game, and his limbs ached and his breath threatened at every stride to fail him. Once he faltered—that was near the fifteen-yard line—and a note of triumph burst into the pandemonium of sound from the watchers. But he struggled on again. The ten-yard line was almost under foot when he felt the shock of the tackle. Grimly he hugged the ball, struggled to advance, did manage to cross the white streak, and then stretched his length on the turf, hunched his head out of danger, and had the last breath driven from his body as the foremost of the pursuit hurled themselves upon him. Somewhere, very, very far away it seemed, a whistle blew. And then he knew nothing more until the big sponge splashed over his face, and he regained consciousness to find them pumping his arms up and down and kneading his chest. He smiled up into Bert's anxious face.

"All right," he murmured faintly.

And in another minute he was back at his end of the line and Bert was telling them that there was only a minute to play, and that they'd got to get through. The ball was eight yards from the last white line and Fairview, desperate and ugly, was between.

"All right, fellows!" shouted Cotton. "Everybody into it! Signal!"

Then Hansel was running back to shove and grunt behind a confused mass at the center of the line. Canvas rasped against canvas, short groans and cries of exhortation filled the air, and somewhere in front Bert, with the ball clasped tightly to his stomach, was fighting inch by inch, foot by foot, toward the goal line. Then something gave somewhere and Hansel went stumbling forward into a confused maelstrom of legs and bodies, while against his ears burst a sudden tempest of shouts. He found his feet, hurled some one, friend or foe, he never knew, from his path, and emerged from the mass of fallen players to see Bert, white and unconscious, lying sprawled upon his back across the goal line with the ball well over.

A goal from that touchdown was too much to hope for. The punt-out failed, and the ball went back to the center of the field. But in a moment it was all over, and the final whistle sounded the defeat of Fairview. And Hansel, on the side line, with Bert's head on his knees grinned foolishly and was very happy. Bert opened his eyes.

"Over?" he whispered weakly.

"All over!" answered Hansel.

Bert sighed again, and again closed his eyes.

"We win," he said faintly.

It was three hours later. Mr. Ames, his hands clasped behind him, was strolling thoughtfully to and fro along the corridor of the first floor of Weeks. In the dining hall, behind closed doors, the football team had gone into executive session in the matter of choosing a captain for next year, and when, in the course of his trips back and forth, he passed the big doorway, the dim murmur of earnest voices met his ears. There is no training-table room at Beechcroft, and the team members dine at one end of the big hall. To-night the other students had been hustled out of the hall very early, and since before seven the football warriors, with the coach, the trainer, and several graduates of prominence, had been in full possession.

There had been broiled chicken and Maryland biscuits and French fried potatoes, and many other luscious dishes served to the players and their guests as extras, for to-night's supper was their "banquet," and if it wasn't as elaborate as the after-victory feasts of some teams, it tasted mighty good to the fellows upon whom the monotonous *régime* of steaks and chops, milk and toast, had begun to pall. After the banquet there had been speeches. The graduates had spoken, Mr. Ames had spoken, Bert had spoken, even Mr. Foote had found a word or two to say. Then they had sung the school song, standing about the long table, and had cheered for Bert, for Mr. Ames, for Mr. Foote, for the manager, for the grads and for Beechcroft. After that the outsiders had gone their ways and the big doors had been closed again.

Down on the green, dark forms moved about in the moonlight, coming from all directions and meeting in the corner of the field sacred to bonfires. Throughout the village wise householders were on the alert, keeping watchful eyes on gates, chicken coops, and like movable and inflammable matter. Now and then a boy stuck his head in the door and looked questioningly and impatiently at Mr. Ames. Outside a group awaited the news; waited, too, to carry off the heroes to the scene of the celebration. Mr. Ames passed the closed doors for perhaps the twentieth time, and looked at his watch. They were taking a long time in there. He wondered whether the election would turn out the way he wanted it to. As he turned again toward the outer door Phin entered and approached him.

"Have they elected a captain yet?" he asked eagerly.

Mr. Ames shook his head.

"Not yet, I think; everything's been pretty quiet in there so far."

"Do you think Hansel has a show?"

"Why not? There's scarcely anyone besides he and Royle that can take it."

"I hope he does get it," said Phin.

"I think he would make a good captain," said the other thoughtfully. "And I think he deserves it." Mr. Ames smiled. "With Dana as captain and you as manager, next year I fancy we'll have a wonderful administration."

"I don't know about that," answered Phin. "In fact, I may not be here. A good deal depends on whether I get a scholarship this year."

"I wouldn't worry about that," answered the instructor dryly. "If a student deserves the money and does his work conscientiously, as you have, the faculty generally looks after him. And there's Cameron. He's in about the same boat with you. But I fancy we'll see you both here next year."

"Cameron? I hope so. I hope he'll be able to play for us, sir. It's been rather hard lines on Cameron, but he took it finely, didn't he?"

"He did, indeed."

"I've been wondering," continued Phin, "how Fairview learned about him. Don't you think some one here gave them a tip?"

"Yes," was the reply. "And I think I know who."

"Who was it?" asked Phin eagerly.

"Well, if you won't let it get any farther, I'll tell you. It was the principal."

"Dr. Lambert?" cried Phin. "Are you sure?"

"Quite. He told me. It was Dana's doing. He went to see the doctor about your absence from recitations, you know, and the doctor got him talking about the football situation. I fancy Dana must have opened the doctor's eyes somehow. At any rate, he's been taking a new attitude ever since. Before this year he's never seemed to care anything about it. Now he's studying up on it. He was at the game this afternoon. He looked rather bewildered when I saw him, but he stuck it out."

"Well—" Phin began. Then he stopped and listened. From behind the closed portals came the sound of clapping hands. He looked questioningly at Mr. Ames. The latter nodded and together they walked toward the door. Then from within came a great cheer:

"*Beechcroft! Beechcroft! Beechcroft! Rah, rah, rah! Rah, rah, rah! Rah, rah, rah! Dana! Dana! Dana!*"

Mr. Ames held out his hand, smiling, and Phin clasped it.

"Success to you both," said the instructor softly.

Then the doors flew open.

THE END